TOUCHING
EVIL

For William Kremer,

with best wishes —

Norma Rosen

TOUCHING EVIL

NORMA ROSEN

Wayne State University Press   Detroit   1990

94   93   92   91   90   5   4   3   2   1

Library of Congress Cataloging-in-Publication Data
Rosen, Norma
Touching evil / Norma Rosen.
p. cm.
ISBN 0-8143-2298-0. — ISBN 0-8143-2299-9 (pbk.)
I. Title.
PS3568.077T68   1990   89-38145
813'.54 — dc20   CIP

The words quoted from "Isle of Capri" are copyright © 1934 by Peter Maurice Music
Co., Ltd. Copyright renewed. Used by permission of T. B. Harms Company.

"Touching evil brings with it the grave peril of succumbing to it. We must, therefore, no longer succumb to anything at all, not even to good."
— Carl Gustav Jung
Memories, Dreams, Reflections

"Our old evil does not comprehend the terror, which begins . . . where our old evil left off. Our old good . . . will do no good. Terror beyond evil and joy beyond good: that is all there is to work with. ⸴ . ."
— Isaac Rosenfeld
An Age of Enormity

Foreword

Touching Evil, first published in 1969, was imagined and written before the late somber flowering of eye-witness Holocaust books of these last few years. It grew not out of research, but out of response to certain works more or less stumbled upon by me in English translation — among others, the recovered diary entries of those who were murdered, a terrifying tome called, as I remember (I have not had the courage to go back to it), *The Black Book of Polish Jewry*, and the televised testimony of survivors at the Eichmann trial which I watched, day by horrifying day. A by no means exhaustive list (that kind of reading would come later), but more than enough to start the landslide of images that became my novel about safe Americans whose minds are wrenched open to the imagining of radical evil in their own time.

Touching Evil is about the Holocaust but there are no living Jews in it, only the shadows of dead ones.

"Since the Holocaust is the central occurrence of the Twentieth Century" — I am quoting here from an essay of mine written shortly afterward — "non-Jews ought to be as obsessed by it as Jews. In my book, at least, they would be."

While writing *Touching Evil* I sometimes called it, to myself, *Heart's Witness*, or *Witness through Imagination*.

As safe Americans we were not there. Since then, in imagination, we are seldom anywhere else.

1990

TOUCHING EVIL

One |

It's not that I forgot you, Loftus. I went down that morning to buy a newspaper. I came back. Strictly back. Checked the mailbox, climbed the two flights to the apartment with the mail and the paper. You know my days. You told me what you thought of them one weekend in bed. We were leaning away from each other . . . sly smiles above the conversation . . . we didn't want to blow up the bridge below . . . you were warming to your subject and nudging for emphasis. It wasn't supposed to have been three weekends before the last. You and Erna were going to get a divorce. You were hard on my days because my days were going to be changed. We knew that.

"What's free," you said, "about free-lance work? It's an illusion of freedom. Especially for a woman. What a price," you said, "you make yourself pay for it. Schedules! Discipline!" You jabbed to make your points. You scanned my face for reactions (psychologist! deducing while seducing) which were part sex, part still protecting my days; you were needling me both ways.

"That's no rhythm for a woman," you said. "Where's your ebb and flow? Your in and out? See?"

It's not that I forgot what you said. The moving finger writ it for me. We were lying on our sides and keeping our bodies, from the waist up, from touching. "I'm taking you away," you said, "from all that. It's only now a question of a little time. You'll have your work," you said. "But you won't have to go at it like a demon. See? Not—like —that—"

Even then, when the bridge blew up and we flew in bits through the air . . . that's what makes sex so lonesome . . . it's the flying . . . it's the damned doubleness of every joy . . . it's all that death and resurrection, and who wants to be a holy ghost . . . even then the coming back to find one senseless afterthought buried under a stone like a survivor of the blast: I will always be able to salvage what is my own.

I have my schedules while you're not here. My disciplines. As you know. When I come upstairs every morning, I drink a second cup of coffee while I scan the paper, look at my mail. I allow myself twenty minutes, no more. After that I'm at my worktable. It's piled with manuscripts and book-jacket material waiting to be designed by me. Business is good. Ebb and flow didn't earn me my reputation. Or in and out. Schedules. Disciplines. You know this is what my life is like. Week after week, while you're not here.

It's not that I forgot you. But that morning, when I came back to the apartment—you know how when you stand in the entryway you can see into the living room and through that into the bedroom—my hands, still holding the mail and the newspaper, started to shake.

A young man—the night before he had been a shivery frog—slept in my bed. On his back, my blanket down to his naked waist. His arms stretched above his head on the pillow. A few matted curls of hair in the armpits. His chest skinny and smooth. His face small and pointy-chinned, his eyelids glossy. His hair not quite peppercorns, but very black and tightly waved. Suggestion of a beginning mustache above his full lips, whitish at the fullest parts. His skin a yellowish tan—Prince Valiant in the morning; with a suggestion of orange tint—Tristan at sunrise.

I said to myself, For Chrissake! and tried, going nearer, to walk like I had Oxfords on. All he is, I said to myself, is city mixture. Mostly poor Puerto Rican boy in New York. A kid, but big enough to be thrown out of school and out of the house. Anyone who wants him can take him home. . . .

He opened his eyes and stared at me, motionless. He said, "I know. You wanna get me outta here."

"There's no special hurry," I said from the bottom of my Oxfords. "I'll work at my desk in the next room. You can sleep if you're still tired."

He looked into the crook of his arm. "I better get up."

I felt his struggle. His life is free-lance, too. Nothing makes it go from outside. So there's always this longing to sink back into softness and sleep. But there's also this terror of drowning if you do. I couldn't think of anything to say that would help him.

He brought his arm down to throw off the covers, then stopped. He remembered he was naked. His clothes were piled on the chair. Last night he was supposed to have slept on the sofa in the living room and I was supposed to have slept in the bed. But I thought, since I've taken him home to give him bed for one night, let him have the bed. I slept on the sofa myself. Except for the time we were together in the bed. He called out of a nightmare, Loftus, and I went to comfort him. Do you believe that? Then he was in me and out of me almost in the count of five. When he was in he went like a locomotive and was finished. I think he was even asleep while it happened. His body felt my body next to it, rolled onto it, and began. What I felt was what you feel when you're on a train, looking out. Strange houses, strange yards. A queer perspective in train experience. Everything seems to be passing through you, not you through it. A passing without contact. What I felt was nostalgia for this place and this moment. Like the light of stars, already past by the time it's perceived. Vaginal nostalgia. Is there such a thing?

I found Jesús at the skating rink. I caught him there. A skinny, frozen fish, underweight and underage. Impossible to throw him back. He needed a place. I swear there was no other motive to my bringing Jesús home but pity for him. Does it look some other way? Let me look. Ah, there you are, Miss Jean Lamb. I see you're approaching the losing side of age, and you live alone? Your lover is held away on weekends now by pressing business? (What the hell are you and Erna *doing*, Loftus?) You pick up a boy in a public place, the way a man picks up a girl. You take him home to your bed.

I swear that wasn't my intention, Loftus. Do you believe me?

Reasons for being at the skating rink? That's because you, Loftus, were delayed (L's abound—I found myself the other morning reciting: My lover, Loftus, of whose letters lately I have lost the file). I try to keep my disciplines and my schedules. But they are slipping away from me. I am distractible now. Just look at the condition of my desk and my file cabinet.

I talk to you all the time now, Loftus, in my mind. A thing I can't do in person or even on the phone any more for a while. I write you letters all the time, the way Hattie writes her letters to me. Except I don't mail mine. Look at this pile from Hattie. Who needs it? I need it. It's a link to you. Who needs a link like that?

For God's sake, Loftus, if I don't tell you Jesús got up and dressed, he stays there, naked, staring at me from my bed. His body is wiry and strong. He draws from his youth the strength and beauty that his diet can't provide. When he is older the vitamin deficiencies of his babyhood will catch up with him (I swear to you, Loftus, the sight of his naked body brings out the dietitian in me as much as anything else. I long to feed him balanced meals. Mrs. Frances Foley Gannett of the Department of Markets in the morning on the radio while I drink my twenty-minute coffee, look at the paper and the mail: "Good morning, housewives—kale and broccoli are abundant in the markets this morning and fish is plentiful; all excellent buys and nourishing for your families as well") and he will shrivel prematurely. When I look at him and think, Puerto Rican boy, he suggests to me the tender, tropical smooth-skinned fruit: mango, papaya, banana. Later, if he makes it to later, he will be callused coconut. He will be ugly and he will have fewer natural enemies.

Two |

You called on a Friday at 4:45 P.M. to say why you weren't coming. How many Fridays ago was that? I remember the hour. Your call came a moment after Hattie's usual call and I was about to leave. But I can't remember how many Fridays ago it was. I kept track for a while; then it depressed me. Saturday morning I woke up bereft, not waking with you. Saturday night I was reasonable, and decided to do all the things I do on Sundays after you leave—an early movie, a hot bath. By Sunday night I could hardly bear the touch of my fingers against my own face. I ran out and started walking, fast, and ended up at Sixty-fifth and Fifth. I hadn't been there in years. I entered Central Park Zoo by night. Have you ever done that? You enter night through the Zoo. Gretel in the dark forest. Hansel is already eaten. Past the empty outdoor cages. The cougar and the elk. Past sleeping grizzlies. Once a woman's arm torn off.

Go through a little dark tunnel. Then the ice rink sparkles within its ring of darkness. Music comes in on a cold breath. A white phonograph record—seen from the path above it—from which the skaters, like so many needles, scrape out the racy organ melodies. The coldness, blackness, strangeness and frigid gaiety of all those strangers circling the rink to one rhythm.

At first the rented skate shoes bruised my ankles. Then the blades reached up from below and cut the soles. The pain numbed itself in the cold. Round and round. I crouched low, keeping my knees loose. I was afraid of falling. A group of teen-aged boys against the fence mocked, "How relaxed!"

Years since I'd skated there. I'd forgotten how to dress for it, too. I hadn't stopped to dress for it. I was still in city stockings and a skirt and only one extra sweater. Myself had flung myself out the door before myself could argue with me. Early April in New York—it's not a place that easily yields any springtime hopes—can still freeze you. The cold hit my thighs and neck, all the unaccustomed exposed places, revived by cold.

A waltz. A polka. A mambo. The skaters cut around me while I plodded on. Never mind. There was the cold and the music, the blackness and the crystal stars. A clash and a zest in the air. The world was carved from the sharp ice blades of the skates. We were on an island of white ice, ringed by the animaled dark, which was ringed in turn by lighted skyscrapers, ringed again by darkness. And over it all a darkness, pierced by islands of ice.

I looked up at the stars and muttered over my wounded feet, "Not me they scorn." But I felt they did. And on top of that, Medea would have scorned me, too, if she could have seen me, with the wind whipping heartfelt tears from my eyes.

I muttered on, "What the hell is one lover to the pitiless

9

stars? What touches those frozen bottlecaps up there?"

And the loud-speaker answered, "Couples only."

I was definitely not a couple. I was going to have to quit.

A spray of ice hit me on the cheek as someone dug his blades in to slow himself. An open leather jacket and a wind-whipped face swirled up, a pair of bare cold hands grabbed mine.

"Couples," he said, and we glided off together before his body had ever fully come to a stop.

Long, powerful strokes on the ice.

"Too fast for you?" he said. "Don't worry," he said. "I'd never let you fall."

I should have said something—anything—right then and there. Something to cut through the power those words had over me at that particular moment. I know what I should have said. "When I fall, nobody can hold me up." But it happened too fast, and the words sank in. I could feel them sinking down through my four or five ages of man to the little empty place in childhood that still waits to be filled up with reassurance—"I'd never let you fall."

I saw he couldn't be more than seventeen and it shamed me. But I hung on to him and his words for dear life. His breath smelled of peppered lemons.

He must have felt me examining him, because he threw a sharp sideways look back. "I thought at first you was a kid," he said.

I caught that one before it could do damage. "Want to stop now and find another partner?"

He shook his head. "I like the music too much to stop. I come to skate. Nothin' else."

I didn't know yet that he never bantered. He spoke seriously always, and it gave a kind of courtesy to everything he said.

We were cross-handed. For the first time I was stroking each blade in full rhythm with the long chords of the song. You know what they play. " 'Twas on the Isle of Capri that I found her / Beneath the shade of an old walnut tree. / O I can still see the flow'rs blooming 'round her, / Where we met on the Isle of Capri. . . ." So fast the body doesn't matter any more. Another kind of flying. A few words rattle in the wind.

"You a teacher?"

"No."

"I thought you was a teacher."

"You go to school?"

"They kick me out."

"Why?"

"I cut up a guy."

We skate, smooth as flowing water. Once, on a train going west—it was the summer before I left college for good and I was visiting my aunt—I sat up at night in the club car thinking of my first lover, John Oates, and looking older than my years. A man started talking to me and pretty soon he said, "Haven't you ever gone to bed with a man—just like that?"

"O no," says I. "I'd have to love him."

"You should try it," says he. "You'd be surprised."

Then he smiled, said good night, and got off at the next stop. So there was nothing in it for him, you might say, but he was like a missionary, spreading the word.

I look at my partner again. "Why did you cut him up?"

"He had it coming. He called me a thief."

"And your parents?"

"My stepfather kick me out."

"Your mother?"

"She busy."

"With what?"

"The little kids."

The music stops. We stop. Still suspended. Filled with cold air and brightness.

"But where do you sleep?"

He shrugs. "With a buddy sometimes. Or my cousin. If it was warmer, in the park." He nods toward the dark outer ring. "A couple of nights, the subway."

"Can you sleep there?"

"Not too good." He is the soul of seriousness. "Anyway, it's singles now," he says, gliding away. He picked up speed and I saw how he could really tear around the rink. Once or twice a guard bumped him to slow him down.

For a while I am back to my aimless round and round. I stop to take off my right skate and rub my foot. Both my feet feel as if the blades are embedded in them. I keep my eye on my partner. As soon as they announce "Couples . . ." I am off like a shot, colliding into him, clutching with my freezing bare hands.

We are cross-armed and flying over the ice again.

"What's your name?"

"Jesús."

I am about to press for his last name, too, but I am afraid he might answer, "They kick me out of my last name."

I tell him only my first name, too. "I'm Jean. I really appreciate your teaching me to skate."

He acknowledges that with a serious nod. "That's okay.

I could teach you to skate because I really love it. I could teach anybody to skate they could be the dumbest person in the world. And that's what I mean about a teacher. Some of these teachers you find, they don't really love their work."

We both keep a long silence after this speech. Which Jesús breaks. "You sure you're not a teacher? You sound like you could be a teacher."

"Me?" I say. "I never even finished school."

For some reason—I know the reason—I was reaching for his sympathy. I didn't mention that it was college I didn't finish. I found myself wishing I could have said, "Me? I used to be a thief." Instead I say that I want to treat us both to hot chocolate.

I bought us each a wedge of pizza with our hot chocolate. When Jesús stopped skating, he looked slight and skinny, an ordinary Puerto Rican boy, sixteen or seventeen, hunched against the cold. He folded up his pizza and took an enormous, bored bite of it.

"Why don't you zip up your jacket, if you're cold?"

"Zipper's broke."

The skin of his throat is tender as a child's. The wind bites at it.

The loud-speaker blares, "Everybody skate!" and I say —so fast that it seems to be the wind that tears the words out of my mouth—"There's a sofa in my apartment. You can sleep on that instead of the subway for a night."

His face shows neither acceptance nor refusal, not even surprise. "I have to talk to my buddies."

"No, don't talk to your buddies. I'm leaving now, if you want to come."

I clump ahead, turn once and see he is following. We

take off our rented skates in the big overheated changing room and turn them in. Then we walk out past the sleeping animals, the hyenas and the monkeys, and take a cab home. On the stairs, I hear Mrs. Jensco's door slam below. But we meet no one.

I show Jesús the bathroom, give him your pajamas and robe. "You can take a shower. There's plenty of hot water."

I make up the sofa with clean sheets and my satin quilt. Then I take a steak from the freezer and put it up to broil for Jesús. While I am cooking it, I think carefully through the contents of the apartment. What is there for a thief to steal? Would he think of strangling me first? (I am disgusted with myself when that nervous-female-all-alone thought occurs. But that doesn't prevent the follow-up idiocy: I could strew my finest pen points on the floor to cut his bare feet.)

Jesús comes out wearing your robe. Of course it's too big. He looks like he's wearing his father's robe. And of course I see him as your son, but never mind that. I serve him the steak and watch him eat.

By the time he is finished, I have decided to give him the bed.

I follow him to the door of the bedroom. "Do you have everything you need?" He nods, then looks back at me over the shoulder of your bathrobe to see if I have left yet. "I'm not wearing no pajamas."

I turn away, and hear him topple into bed. I wash the dishes and the broiler. When I finish I look in on him. Jesús is asleep, his lips parted, his long eyelids glossy as polished pecan shells.

I took a quick shower myself then, and tumbled onto the sofa. I was peaceful for the first time since you'd called to say you were not coming. Although, my God, when I think of it, I brought Jesús home less than forty-eight hours after you called. Knowing that, do you believe me that it was innocent? Because I had already, in anticipation, lived through weeks.

Once I read a story about a man put into a dark, solitary cell with no food, only a candle, which he didn't want to light, for fear of using it up. After a while he figured out how many days must have passed and he was being starved to death. So he broke the candle up into meals. Every once in a while he ate another meal. When all the meals were eaten he lay down to die. Then they came for him. He found he had only been in prison . . . I forget, it was Anatole France or one of those giant French writers—you know how my reading is. You told me once that if anthologies weren't so popular with publishers, and if I hadn't gotten some to design (and to read, skimming, while I worked on them) I never would have got to know a word of any written classic. That shocks you, because I went to college. But I told you, Loftus, I read psychology if I read anything, and not even that too well. Because John Oates was college for me, you know that. Anyway, this giant French writer—unless it was an Italian or a German writer —it was one of these GREAT WORKS OF WORLD LITERATURE things, and I remember I did a kind of massive, architectural lettering for the jacket to suggest how dependable and durable it all was, ha-ha (though on second thought it must have been French or Italian—the Germans wouldn't even have given him a candle). Whoever this writer was, he let out the news at the end of the story—he put it into some terrific language that's supposed to make your flesh creep, but which gets lost in translation, as they say—that this guy was only there about forty minutes or something, maybe an hour.

What's that got to do with Jesús? How the hell should I know? I felt alone in the dark and I rushed us ahead in my mind, months ahead it felt like, and you weren't coming.

The thing is, I didn't even have to pick up a magazine the way I've always had to do during the week, even between your weekends. I just put out the light and felt myself falling asleep.

Then there was the thumping overhead. I turned over and recognized the sounds. The upstairs neighbor's son, who gets nightmares. Sostana. You met her once and later I told you about him. He gets up and pounds the floor with his bare feet and throws himself around, while he sleeps.

I got up. I walked barefoot and stiff to the bedroom. Jesús was crying in his sleep. "Get offa me, you fuck! Get the fuck offa me!"

"Ssh, Jesús." My hand on his arm. "It's all right." He goes on crying.

Lie down beside, stroke his head, get under the covers, put arms around. Feel every bone in his hard, bony, cold body, smell the peppered, sour smell of his breath. "Ssh, it's all right."

Then, without opening his eyes, he rolls onto me. In one stroke in me (did my legs just gape open in surprise, or was I helping? I'm really asking you, I've no idea), in four strokes—to the rhythm of the thumping overhead: thump, thump, thump, thump—finished, out and (still?) asleep.

I lie on my back staring up at the ceiling. Should I jump up, run into the bathroom and douche? Could I catch up with his sperms, speed skater that he is? I see them zooming up the tubes (stop thief! but he's not taking, he's giving), hard heads pecking like duck bills at the egg. No. Too late. I swear my legs were like logs. I simply couldn't move. Besides, you once told me that it was impossible, and never to rely on it. That was, I guess, about when I first started to talk about wanting a child and my age and about how there wasn't all that much time suddenly any more and I guess you got nervous that I might jump the gun (and it had occurred to me to shoot a little hole in the diaphragm—why didn't I do it? I'd already jumped so many guns, I was afraid this one might blast me in the back).

I stared at the darkness overhead. There was no more thumping there. I thought, Sostana and I have quieted the children's nightmares. I listened to Jesús' breathing, then got up and limped back. It was the skating, not Jesús, that had given me the Charley horse.

In the morning I went down, as I said, while he was still asleep. I suppose I felt the best way to handle that particular morning was to go through with my usual routine. I wasn't shocked at myself, don't think that. I could foresee us talking about all this calmly when you came. And most likely in bed. All the same, when I came up with the newspaper and the mail and I saw him all over again, for no reason—there must have been some reason—my hands began to shake.

So then I make breakfast for Jesús. He takes another hot shower meantime, his second since the evening before. And while I cook, I mull over the doubleness of my feelings for Jesús. Both motherly and sexual—open-ended, so to speak.

What is the difference between Jesús, my son, and Jesús,

my lover? I say this to myself while I baste the eggs. The difference in our ages, for example, would not make Jesús any crueler to me as a lover than he would be as a son. He could say the same things: "Listen," he could say, "I don't have to do what you think. You're not the boss of me!" Or, "Your generation loused everything up and it's finished now. This is a new scene, dig?"

The separating break from either son or lover would come at the same moment: when he is drafted. It is now 1961. That is, eight years, I start figuring to myself, since the Korean War ended in 1953, and that started five years after the end of World War II, which started twenty-one years after the end of World War I, or fourteen years before the end of the subsequent war. I start to work it out. I know something about faked geometric progressions, as you know. The point is, I was figuring out that even though the Korean War was over before Jesús came of draft age, the chances were not impossible that a new war would come along in time to accommodate him. And so, even in the matter of the separating break he would, as lover, leave me in the same way he would if he were my son.

Having reasoned through all this I immediately, while the eggs were in the pan staring up through the membranes like embryos' eyes, felt those five plunging thumps. So although there was still some cover-up confusion in my mind, there was none at all in my body about the difference between a lover and a son.

I could think of nothing to say while he silently ate the eggs. Then, when he was ready to go, I gave him your blue muffler to wear and ten dollars to put in his pocket. Everything is a parody of something.

"Any time you want to come back, Jesús . . ."

He looks at the floor.

". . . If you want to take a hot shower, or need a place to sleep . . ."

His eyes on the floor.

"Are you going to look for a job?"

On the floor.

Suddenly, whether it's because of those embryo eyes of the eggs, or the false progression I've cooked up, I give birth to a flood of words.

"Take care of yourself, Jesús. . . . Don't let your buddies give you any bad advice . . . what I mean is don't you *take* bad advice from them . . . you don't have to do what your buddies do . . . you're an intelligent boy (what makes me think that?) . . . I know you're an *honest* boy (or that?) . . . and you're a likable boy (is it that?) . . . and you can do a lot with your life (how do I know?) . . . you can go back to school and get a good job (what makes me think that?) . . . you can save yourself, they could end up in jail. . . ."

He gives me a serious look that says I knew you was a teacher. Too late, I recognize maternal feeling, badly timed. Jesús looks ready to choke, as if food is pushing itself down the passageway meant for air. . . .

"Thanks for the ten dollars," he says, and drums softly down the stairs in his sneakers.

Three |

But on an ordinary morning, Loftus, you know there's no boy in my bed.

Here I am—see?—wrestling mail loose from my box. Manuscripts, junk. Letters of contract: "Dear Miss Lamb, This is to confirm our telephone conversation regarding the Dirkson and Johnson medical text which you have agreed to . . ." Jacket proofs. Galleys. Digging out the tough Manila folders. First approach to the mailbox is intuitive. I smell what's in it. I smell there's no letter from you, Loftus. My knuckles are skinned. Here is another chapter from Hattie . . . sucking at my knuckle . . . drowning me in her life. Everything drops. Hattie's chapter rips open on the mailbox lid. My knuckle sheds blood on it. A note clipped to the top of this installment. Fifteen pages aren't enough for her; she clips on afterthoughts, too. "Jean, do you exist? Did I invent you because I need you . . . are you real . . . ?"

Bulky envelopes slip from my skinned fingers; I am pumped fuller of details about Hattie's life than I can remember of my own. And she asks if I'm real.

Remember, Loftus, you're the one who put Hattie on my trail. Remember all these things.

Now up the two flights to the apartment—see? Drop all the stuff on my desk. The installment of Hattie's life bursts open and I grab it to get over with whatever I'm going to read of it. Sure enough: "I feel I am bursting through membranes, as the baby will burst through mine. . . . I am in other people's lives more than I am in my own. . . . I have the *illusion* of breaking through into other people's lives, sometimes into your life, Jean, I have the illusion of living in your life. Your work, your neatness, your order, the way your hands move (you have spoon-shaped nails, did you know that?) over your papers, the work on your desk, giving shape. O alone! Dignified and austere . . ."

How do you like that, Loftus?

I am shuddering to think Hattie will burst through the membrane separating her life from mine. I do not want her in bed with us, Loftus, when you come again. I don't even want her sitting up with me week nights at my worktable, either (yes, I do that now), when I am tranquilizing myself with calligraphy like an illuminating monk.

A part of almost every letter from Hattie, aside from her membranological responses, is a little history of her short past. She is trying to establish her own reality in me. No recollection is too petty: ". . . and I can remember how green the trees were, how blue the sky seemed in Fairmont, how much I loved that little town. But I loved Ezra more and I gladly left it to come to New York with him. Now, sometimes, I don't know who or what I love. Did I imagine love, too?"

Hattie's letter lands on my own piled-up papers on

that desk she thinks so orderly, and which grows more disorderly with every week you don't come. (I have to admit —it got disorderly all at once. Maybe that has something to do, but I don't exactly know what, with the story about the man who started starving the minute he thought there was a chance he might be going to starve.) I have a collection of Hattie's letters—her manuscripts—stuffed in a drawer. If I threw them away? Must I keep every damned bloody one of them?

I give the whole thing a shove. And am rewarded with a sight of the blue envelope. There *is* one! It had been hidden, sat on by Hattie's life. Your college-blue stationery, the same as that used by the undergraduate women, looking outwardly prim. The flap's undone. Sealed up in haste, it must have been, like a surprised lover. I pounce on it with joy.

". . . Miss you, my darling. I *have* written to Erna to push for the divorce . . ." (My God, it's an *old* letter!) ". . . This way is stupid. With your decency and kindness and strength—you can't know how much I value them in you—you've tried to spare me this confrontation, but I won't put it off any more. The stupidity! Erna writes back so reasonably it makes me ashamed. Why did I put it off? That makes it harder for everyone. She does try basically to be decent and basically to be kind. How she succeeds is another matter. When she is frightened . . . but then how we all succeed is another matter. She says she will come up to the college one weekend to go over everything about the divorce. I tried to talk her out of it. I said letters and lawyers ought to be enough, since we've had no reason to see each other at all for over a year. She insists. Maybe she's right. Maybe it's best. We'll get it over with in one unpleasant visit. I don't know when it will be. Meantime I'll see you this weekend, thank God. All my love. . . . P.S. Have you persuaded Hattie to stop watching yet? Or have you gotten drawn in, too? Darling, I worry about you getting drawn in. . . ."

I stare at your letter, which I've read before. I see again your wife, Erna, whom I've never seen, walk toward you, embrace you, kiss your lips. You look pained to see pain on her face. "I never meant to hurt you, Erna, never!"

I take your letter to my file cabinet.

Is it shocking that I keep your letters in a file? Cold-blooded? But where should I keep them, then? My life is paper. Paper drowns in paper on my desk. See what happened to your letter that I didn't file. And see what happens to Hattie's letters, which I never file. I never meant to save them. But I can't bring myself to throw them away. They are stuffed in a desk drawer—the ones that aren't floating on my desk—hatching out reality from idealized bits of remembered small-town life, from fears of now. . . .

Now then, check the L folders. L for lover and Loftus alike. The last letter (if it is the last letter, and if it's in its rightful place) lies at the front of the folder. "It drives me mad . . ."—jumps out— ". . . why things can't happen faster than they happen. But I can't help that . . . Darling, be patient. . . ."

No, that must certainly be out of its proper order. I would remember it in a different way if it really were the most recent. It's undated. Unaddressed, too, come to that. "Darling—" But there have been other darlings. In your life as well as mine. And it's typed. I don't recognize the typescript. Mine? An unsent letter? Yours? A former lover's?

Is it possible or worthwhile to trace typescript? But there's no need to complicate private life with fantasies about the public life of one's time—see Hiss vs. Chambers—is there?

It's only hard to wait and to keep things in place during the waiting. See, even your letter popped out of its place. That's all I mean . . . that's the kind of thing. . . .

File the letter. Shut the file. Back to my desk.

A new novel by a Nobel Prize winner. I am entrusted with that. For the dignity of my calligraphy. A high school textbook with sixteen-page picture insert—that pays the rent. Maybe I will start to design Hattie's letter without knowing it. More like a manuscript than a letter from someone who lives across the street.

It is now 9:30. I will work till 4:45. About that time Hattie's phone call will come. A reminder. A few minutes before five I will go across the street to her apartment to watch the Eichmann trial with her on her television set. I begin to shake and sweat as I walk across the street. Although the truth is I don't any longer give a damn. It is absolutely established practice. I can't get out of it. I went once, twice, thinking, no more. Now I am drawn in. And all for you, Loftus. Though you wished me not drawn in. You wanted me drawn in so you could feel you were helping Hattie, and you also wanted me not drawn in so that you needn't worry that you were injuring me. You are the one who is decent and kind, and this is as far as even your decency and kindness can go.

Listen, Loftus! I am up to my ears in Hattie's life, in her husband, Ezra's, and her sister's and her sister's husband's! What I don't witness for myself when I am with them, Hattie sends me in these letters—these chapters from her life, these "how-things-were-with-me-then" and "how-I-feel-about-it-all-now" letters.

And I'm up to my ears again in corpses. Those same flesh-less bones that fell on me seventeen years ago. I know now there's nothing to do but heave them off. But they're fall-ing on Hattie for the first time, and I'm with her. . . .

Is it any wonder there are episodes for me in Central Park? What is one little Puerto Rican boy in the sightless eyes of all those corpses!

No more episodes, Loftus! I want no more installments, no broken-off chapters, no more asterisks! Loftus, stitch up my life! Make these fragments into a book!

For your sake, Loftus, I allow myself to be drowned in all this now. Soon, like flying fish, we'll leap up—Loftus, won't we—from these treacherous deeps?

Four |

When I told you about Hattie's letters, her manuscripts really, the journal of her life in one-thousand-and-one installments you said, for a joke, "Why don't you counter-diary her?"

Of course you know about my diary. You know every piece of paper on my desk. Since you've stopped coming, I don't keep my diary at night any more, to knit up the day. I write it in the morning—on ordinary mornings. My ordinary morning hours are full of ruses to involve me in the day. Two paragraphs are what I allow myself, maximum.

I write, *Loftus says*.

This morning I write: *Loftus says that the fable of Pandora's box is no warning against curiosity (not even the curiosity of women like me). It's a warning not to hope the garbage of the world won't dump itself on our heads. . . .*

I've set my loose-leaf journal on my desk on a pile of waiting manuscript. I can feel myself covering layers of words with more layers.

. . . We are always telling ourselves we only want to

peek, Loftus says, only to play—for a minute. Who wants consequences? Responsibilities? They come, but not because we have peeked or played. It's truer to say it the other way. We peeked or played so they could come. Tiny wombs and openings develop in the bodies of fetal girls, Loftus says, so that at the proper time destiny may have its door. . . .

I read that and all it tells me is that I am obsessed with the idea of having a child—which I already knew (but not that I wanted it to be a daughter).

All the same, the diary has served its purpose. I'm awake. I'm in the day. Ready to go out for paper and mail. In a way the summons from Hattie at nearly five, the one that brackets my working day at the other end, is also an impetus to begin the day.

But the least crutch, the flimsiest ruse, the driest sort of discipline—like having to get up in the morning in order to write a bare two paragraphs in a journal—even that can become a dependency. Overwhelming temptation to go on to paragraph three.

When I've time (you can see I'm frightfully busy) I must letter a sign to tack above my desk. PUT AWAY DIARY NOW.

Hattie's syndrome has taken hold of me. I want to see how my life will fit into words. This is what Hattie must feel. . . .

Here's how it began. . . . (Against my will I am writing again.) *A weekend ending. And in that atmosphere of time collapsing, and Loftus picking through his things, preparing to leave, suddenly snapping back his head in that self-berating way he has* (did you know—as Hattie asks me —you do that?)—*"I almost forgot to tell you," said Loftus,*

"I met a former student of mine. She lives right here, on your street somewhere. On Friday as I was coming up the street myself. She was in my class three years ago. She was one of the town girls. An independent little thing. Now she's married and pregnant, O Lord, how pregnant . . . it was a shock. . . ."

That haunted house I take to be my womb tightens. (I write that. How satsifying! Probing the toothache with my tongue. Tapping the uterus with my pen.) *Loftus' laugh is easy. He goes on. "All the same, big belly or not, it didn't stop her from one of those earnest student questions. You know. 'Professor Genarian, as a <u>psychologist, how do you account for the evil in the world?</u> How do you account for life being the way it is?'"*

"O what did you say? O poor Loftus."

"I said I couldn't account for a damn thing. I said I had lived through this whole business the first time news of it came around and I didn't know any more now than I did then. She's watching the Eichmann trial on TV, you see, darling, and I felt so damn sorry for her. Had a glimpse of a frightened child who's turned on the horror movie and doesn't know how to turn it off. So I gave her your phone number instead. <u>Watch with her if you can</u> sometime, darling?"

"O of course darling, no not a bit not at all. . . ."

"<u>Or talk her out of watching altogether, better yet.</u> <u>What's the good of watching—a child like that.</u> And now she's going to have a child. She'll have to keep a grip on her joie de vivre if she's going to do her baby any good. The horrors of the monster's cave are no preparation for motherhood, tell her that, will you? It didn't occur to me to say it at the time. . . ."

28

While Loftus was telling me this, and putting one sock on, and then sitting with it hanging limp from his toes, I felt that someone had given out a chapter of my life. One of the early passages was being parodied. But Loftus would not do that. He has come with his kindness and decency late into my life (no! thirty-six isn't late; only forty or forty-two is; or forty-three) to show me that the responses I had found too painful to make must in any case be made (sometimes even forty-four . . . I believe I've heard of forty-five. . . .) What doesn't catch you early catches you late. (But forty is late enough.)

All along it was understood that I was the one who was supposed to say the word. I thought of saying the word ("Now! I need to have a child now!")—of the whole process—as one of those old Rube Goldberg cartoons. I would say the word to Loftus. That was (A). He would tell it to his wife (B). She would somersault into the air, causing the bucket suspended above (C) to overturn, drenching us all in (D)—what?

At that point I balked. I did not want to know whether that was really only cartoon blood in (C). But a breeze from somewhere, the stress of the air waves themselves, set the comical mobile in motion. (D) has drenched us all right. Now we are all down on hands and knees groping in the slime. And one of us has accidentally touched the lever (E). A small white rat runs out, like a streak of enlightenment. Which we are pursuing. . . .

I don't like this, Loftus. I look at everything put down here and I don't like it at all. If I ever sent this to Hattie or to anyone, I'd be sending the wrong life.

Even so, I don't stop. I reread the diary entry. Now I have the feeling I am glimpsing a piece of someone's novel, the way I do when I turn pages of a manuscript to be designed:

Jean and Loftus spent the last afternoon of their weekend in bed, as they always did. They got up to have brunch in the kitchenette, went back to bed, talked about his wife and decided again there was no need to push a divorce on her—in bed—she had said she would agree to one, she just wanted to get used to the idea. Loftus' wife, sustained by whatever shadowy traces of marriage are left—in bed— she had never asked for a divorce—has a job and an apartment in another city. Loftus feels a divorce is possible now —in bed—morally right for the first time. His children are old enough to understand, his wife has another life— in bed—he loves Jean, and Jean's time is running out. . . . In bed . . .

I catch sight of my desk clock. I need another sign. IF YOU CAN'T KEEP YOUR DIARY ON SCHEDULE, DON'T KEEP ONE AT ALL. I dress to go out. When you're leaving, Loftus, to catch your train back to the college in Fairmont, four hours away, you know how I dress like a house afire. I always have to walk out the door with you. While I dress, you hunt up a movie for me. That weekend you told me about Hattie you picked *The Life of Michelangelo.*

I barely look in the mirror when I'm dressing to go out with you. I don't like my face then, pale and doubting. But that weekend you told me about Hattie, I caught myself looking. A little puffed from love-making. Without make-up, rubble beginning to collect under the eyes —the years bombard you, anyhow, all the while you think you're in your shelter. How could I ever have thought there was time? I caught myself thinking: No gray yet, thank God; thank God I'm not a blonde, they dry out faster; thank God I've got one of those long cheek-bones-and-chin faces, they keep your muscles pinned into place a few years longer than the heart-shaped lovelies I'd have given so much to resemble in my youth.

Women my age browse at department store make-up counters among the soothing creams and colored powders. Could you insert a little of the Queen Bee Royal Jelly up there, please, I'd like to say sometime. I have a feeling it's going terribly dry and wrinkled and patchy. Even if they're only laugh lines, it can't be getting any younger, can it? The eggs may start falling from the uterine lining like so many dried sycamore seed balls.

I remember I said, "Artistic films don't do for me on Sunday nights."

"*Butterfield 8*? That's playing near Grand Central."

". . . Or other women's messy lives . . ."

"Is your life messy?" You were preparing to be hurt . . .

In the bathroom, slapping powder on a pale, puffed face, I groaned to the mirror.

"What?" You squeezed your face in to see, too.

"How could I not have known I was nailed to the days of the week?"

"A curse on the days of the week and on their nails."

"Do you think in there looks tired?" I put my hand on the bottom of my belly.

"You?" You smoothed over the place. "No wrinkles anywhere. You're lovely. But a curse on the weeks and the years we didn't know each other, anyway. That little pocket in there could have held dozens of children. But there's time, there's plenty of time. You're only thirty-five!"

(Did you know I lied?)

"But then your own children wouldn't have been born. . . ."

"O—" You braced your foot on the tub, checked shoe-laces needlessly—"they would have, somehow—"

Now they were late. They must rush. In the novel I have glimpsed . . . in bed . . . in a final love-making they felt, in the thudding of their hearts (they never had to consult the clock; it was what made their Sunday love-making overly tender and never lustful enough) that it was time . . . in bed . . . for him to catch his train. . . .

"Where are you sending me after your train leaves?"

You went with comic haste once more to the newspaper. "Yes, madam's movie schedule!"

You were relieved I was no longer gloomy. It's not for *that* you wanted to marry again. Why should a man with grown children worry about babies? Why should you care whether my womb is young or old?

"No, honestly, darling, it doesn't matter. I'll just go for a little walk this time after your train leaves. I'll come back and go to sleep early-early and before I know it, it's morning and I'm up and at work."

We both looked at my desk where the tissue layouts were neatly stacked (still, at that time) under the *millefleurs* paperweight you gave me.

"Do that!" How relieved you were. In the cab you said, "Do get to bed early, darling." Automatically I thought, it shows if I don't get my sleep.

"I could kick myself now for what I blurted out to that girl, that what's-her-name, Hattie Mews," you said. "The last thing in the world you want is to hear the troubles of a frightened pregnant child. I should never have given her your phone number. . . ."

"Oh no, I don't mind. . . ."

"I mind! It was a damned silly stupid thing to do. That's all you need, a frightened schoolgirl mother-to-be leaning on you. She's got a husband here, anyhow, and a married sister who can check on her. . . . But no, I had to contribute my bit. . . . I couldn't resist that appeal to my protection. . . ."

"It doesn't matter. I've been there and back, too."

"No, you haven't. You're too young to say that about yourself."

"I'm not that young."

"Well, I'm forty-eight. Going on forty-nine. You only say that because people have leaned on you."

"You haven't."

"Yes, I leaned on you, too, giving her your phone number. I didn't know what to say to her . . . her face all swollen and mottled in that mother-to-be way. I felt simply stricken when she asked me that question. So I gave her your phone number . . ."

"O no . . ."

"There's no self-pity in you," you said, as we walked down the ramp to the cinder-smelling track. "You don't know what a blessed breeze that is in the desert."

"I want you to lean . . ." I shaped that with my lips as your train pulled away.

I went to a revival of *The Thirty-nine Steps*. But first the newsreel came on. There again was the courtroom and the trial in progress. There was the functionary, Eichmann, on trial with his manuscripts. Checking out for accuracy the accounts of the monster's caves. Mentally I reached out for that mess of papers through which he endlessly shuffled. I wanted to grab them and order them—put big bold headings on and set off the technical material in nice readable small type with plenty of white space between the lines—I'm a functionary, too. And there were the witnesses shuffling, without the aid of manuscripts, through their memories. Trying, without hope of success, to tell how it was to die of the horror in the monster's caves.

Later, at the sight of beautiful Madeleine Carroll (now an aging, fattening housewife in Britain—was it possible? —aging, aging, you haven't a self-pitying bone in your body that isn't aging), I burst into tears and left. . . .

But while your train pulled out you were smiling, Loftus, and kissing a finger to me. You loved seeing me brave and gallant. Why shouldn't you? I loved seeming it.

But if I sent any of this to Hattie, I would be sending the wrong life, do you *see* that?

Five |

Tonight my downstairs buzzer sounds at nearly mid-night. The first signal, and then my answering one, rip through the quiet of the house.

Soft padding of sneakers up the stairs. Jesús stands with his hands grasping the edges of his black jacket, holding his short, slender body in a dancer's alertness.

"I need a place," he says, his grave voice full of doubt.

He lives in momentary responses. If I hesitate, he will be off, springing lightly down the stairs and thinking, I knew she was a teacher.

I open the door wide.

"Come in."

Another hot shower. A long one. And then a long time knocking things about in the bathroom after the water is shut off. He even begins to sing a little in a swingy bari-tone: "When you gon' to make me your very own. . . ."

I knock at the bathroom door. "Here is a good big towel for you, Jesús."

He opens, smiles ruefully at its soft towelly whiteness. "Ah, you shoulda tol' me that before. I jus' use the one you got hangin' here."

In the medicine chest mirror I can see his straight muscular back, the small buttocks whitened with my talcum powder.

He sees me looking. "You don' min' if I use some a your stuff, do you?"

"I don't mind." I step past him and into the shower stall as I am, toss my clothes to the floor from behind the bubbled glass door, and drown my body in steaming water. When I shut off the water, I say, "Now let me have the white towel, please, Jesús."

Jesús reaches his arm around behind the partly open shower door.

"Now powder."

When my body is as clean and hot and sweet-smelling as his, I open the door and step out. I stand very still while Jesús looks at me and I can see it is probably true that he doesn't hate his mother. Probably he would love her if he had the chance. But he will not touch me first.

While he is slowly rising—his gravity goes deep—I feel a great sigh coming up in my chest. As it comes up my breasts swell and Jesús watches that. Then my breath comes slowly out between my lips and Jesús watches my mouth. Then he raises his eyes and lets me see the great, grave longing in them. I take his hand and we walk together to my bed.

When we are together, he fragrant above me so that I feel I am lying under an arching branch of some young fruit tree, Jesús looks as if he is about to begin pondering something. I whisper, "Don't *wonder* about me, Jesús. Do what you like to do."

What he likes to do is Go-Man-Go!

Six |

But on ordinary mornings, I step out the front door, go down the four stone steps and take an appreciative breath of the dirty air. I breathe it in, whatever it is. I am only going up the street, Loftus, around one treacherous corner and back.

This morning a well-dressed man passes me as I step out. He is like a walker in a dream, blind to other walkers. He watches where he puts his feet. In this neighborhood, curbstones disappear overnight. The brownstones and low apartment houses on the street—like mine or the one where Hattie lives—might have turned into something else or disappeared altogether by the time the well-dressed man returns from work. Four floors, front fire escapes freshly painted orange. Vanished. X'd away.

The man wears a hat, carries an attaché case and a slim, furled umbrella. The sky is brilliant, but a storm is promised.

A little farther on, the cement sidewalk gives way to a raised boardwalk. I go three steps up, walk along a platform, then three steps down and across a puddle with a plank in it. The path turns a sharp corner left and grows walls made of blue and yellow and pink doors, with here and there a doorknob in the wall. There is an opening in the wall at the left. I pass the vast, empty space that is to be the lobby of the concrete building that is being poured upward, now at its twelfth story. In there, houses within the house. A small dark shack at the back—Johnny on the Spot. A largish green wooden house, with windows and even a chimney stack with a triangular metal cap on it. Two or three fires blazing in cans. A stench of wetness creeps out. The faces of the men in there are dark with the darkness of a cave.

A laborer crosses my path at the end of the corridor of doors. He supports on his shoulder a very long, slim metal pipe and as he walks, one hand on his hip, the two ends dip toward the ground and bob up again, flexible as bamboo.

"Watch!" he calls, his voice abstract, like a street crier's. "Watch!"

Up in the air a sunburned man preens himself and whistles. His companion treads air, calls down, "Barbara? Marie? Dolores? Look up!" And the first man sings down, "Honey? Sweetheart?"

I fight down blushing and a desire to giggle. After all, an inner voice reminds me. Nearly forty. Certainly not, another voice protests. Thirty-six at most.

Still, when the men call to me the springs of my body are ready to gush as if nothing that has been has ever been. A moment of sheer, physical delight, like being tickled. I smile and wave up. The chaos of the street revives for a moment the myth of the virile, joyful worker. Passing that part of the street has a cheerful, Italianate heat. Then that blows off again like dust.

The next is a broken-faced brownstone, where Negro wreckers carry baskets of plaster from the wreck to a truck that is equally a wreck, its sides concocted from bits of the building. In contrast to the booming machinery of construction, the work of housing destruction is of another era, a hand-picking of plaster and board. Because I have just gone, gushing springs, through my Italian street scene, I feel the silent, dead moment between my Negro countrymen and me. I try to bestow my nod of friendship, but there are no eyes on me to catch it.

Construction again. This is poured concrete. Two stories up, the men are dancing in the slime. They call down that I am gorgeous. I mean to give them a wave, to show I like their joke. But the black wreckers have taken the edge off innocent merriment.

When I moved to this neighborhood, the East Fifties in Manhattan, Third Avenue was just beginning its change from a flickering street of bums and commerce. That was before your time, Loftus. That was in Vincent's time. Does that sound cold-blooded? I'm sorry if it does. But my files, if they're still in some kind of order, will bear me out. And I've willed it all to you—my files, my papers, God help you, everything—in case anything should happen; in case, let's say, one of the girders of progress should fall on my head. I told you that, didn't I?

Anyway, they were taking the El down and every new finger of sunlight that poked through the El's broken scaffolding was like a golden dagger on a pirate's map: "Dig here." And dig they did—the money boys were on to the newest treasure, post-World War II land boom. White X's were painted on windows to show vacated apartments. A few faces still looked out of windows between the X'd-out ones. Talk was beginning to be heard in the grocer's and shoemaker's stores on Second Avenue about where the little shopkeepers and cheap-rent families could go. No place, was the conclusion. The wrecking still goes on.

I turn the corner and am on Second Avenue. The store windows in the buildings where the apartments above have already been X'd out are full of little good-by signs.

"Thanking all our customers for thirty years . . ."

It's taken too long, but at last I'm at my destination. My landlady's stationery store on Third Avenue. So far I am in luck. The building where Mrs. Jensco rents her store is not to be sold. She claims that as long as the building where she has her business is not sold she will never sell the one we live in. She and her husband originally bought it years ago as an investment for their savings and a place to live. Now it is worth many times more than they paid.

Mrs. Jensco, a cheerful soul, has her own pun for the whole thing. "It's all just paper profit if you don't sell That's how we began. Paper. We started out selling news-papers, and believe me we won't give it up. I'm no specula-tor." Mrs. Jensco's husband still delivers papers at seven in the morning to everyone in our building but me. News-papers are her special domain. She reads them, too.

She hands me mine now with a look of revulsion on her face.

"It's terrible to read the papers these days," Mrs. Jensco says. "Are you following the trial?"

"Yes." I glance at what's come in new in the lending library, partly to see how many of *my* books are there. "I'm following it."

"What can anybody do with people like that? Hanging's too good."

"Yes," I say.

"I forget, Miss Lamb. Do you have a television set? I can't watch the trial because I'm in the store that hour. But imagine actually seeing those survivors!"

"No," I say, "I don't keep a television in the apartment."

"I see what you mean. Because you work at home and all. You have to keep it like an office."

Mrs. Jensco knows about you, Loftus. For everyone's peace of mind, she stresses the regularity of my life.

"Suppose you had a television set," she says. "And there was something going on. Like a political convention or another thing like those McCarthy hearings, or like this trial. You'd want to turn it on. Then you're an artist, you're visual. So you'd want to look. I can see how you'd have to fight. Anybody working at home like you do has got to be disciplined, I can see that. It's amazing how you do it. I suppose in the morning when you get up you have to put it to yourself. You probably have to say to yourself, 'Well, now, are you going to get up or are you going to stay in bed and go down the drain?'"

"You're right, Mrs. Jensco," I tell her. "Except I say, 'Down the drown.' It scares me more."

"It's amazing how you do it," Mrs. Jensco says graciously, concentrating on my diligent days and leaving to darkness my evening star. That's you, Loftus.

I head for home with my newspaper.

"Jean!"

I turn my head and see it's Hattie. She is across the street, making her way toward me around a dump truck and a huge steel-cable spool. She walks with great slowness and care, her belly pushing out at the front of her raincoat. (The chorus up in the air yells, "Careful, honey . . . easy . . . watch your step!") She has a *babushka* over her straight, long hair and no make-up, either. A wire shopping cart bumps along behind her. I am surprised to see her out so early. She has morning sickness most days, or whatever the late-pregnancy equivalent of that is.

"I saw you through the window!" She is out of breath. "I wondered if you might be going in there, too." She nods at the Chinese laundry shop—"I have to get our bundle and I hate to go in. . . ."

The Chinese laundry has instructions lettered on shirt cardboard stuck in the window: PICK UP LAUNDRY LAST DAY TOMORROW 4:30. GOOD-BY. Tomorrow is today.

I nod yes. I do have to go in and pick up my few sheets. None of your shorts or underwear this time, Loftus. Not for a while now.

Hattie stares at me. In the last few weeks her eyes have begun to pop, like her belly. "He reminds me—" she whispers—"of the—you know?—the Muslims! I can't bear—somehow—to see him."

Then she blushes, looks down at the broken sidewalk, mutters, "I don't know *why* I can't bear to see him. . . ."

We go in. The laundryman is a tall, skeletal Chinese, who stands all day at his iron, which is plugged into the ceiling light. He wears a T-shirt with a number of holes in it; his long arms are nothing but linked bones, and his working elbow sharpens itself in the ironing. His fingernails are ridged and thick like oystershells, tinted blue. His building, an ancient, green-corniced one, is coming down.

In winter he greets his customers, "Col', ah?" In summer, "O boy, warm!" Now he smiles a gummy Chinese smile as he hands each of us our laundry bundle. Hattie's bundle looks as pregnant as she does. Mine looks flat and infertile. All the same, I can appreciate the Chinese package-making art—the brown paper that just meets, the thinnest string that just makes it to a bow and that will pop as soon as it is tugged, the orange ticket with its big number and wonderfully black calligraphed symbol.

In his cadaverous face his teeth are oversize. Under his long, sticklike legs, his feet are ludicrously big. A glance at Hattie, and I can almost see her misplacing him among the near-corpses of last evening's televised trial. She has laid him on the freezing shelves at night with the Muslims— the concentration camp name for those whose will to live had gone, and who drew their shreds of blankets to themselves for comfort like infants.

We both have our legacy from this week's trial. She has her Muslims, I have my corpse-digger.

"Good-by, good-by." The laundryman nods and smiles as if his fortune were good.

Hattie draws her fat bundle along in her cart; I carry my skinny one under my arm. "I also thought I'd stop in . . ." Hattie nods in the direction of the local fruit-and-vegetable store, and then looks at me hopefully.

"I could use some oranges," I say.

Around the corner from the laundry, in the same building, and it's closing too, but without any good-by signs. The narrow panels of the glass-and-wood doors are folded back, this way, that, accordioned, and let in the still chilly air. At the doorway Hattie takes a deep breath, as if inhaling the desolate, crateless look of the store, where nothing had ever been put in for decoration or comfort but crates and bushel baskets.

The vegetable man wears a thick turtle-neck sweater against the chill of his open-fronted store. He is at least enough of a potato or pasta eater. His face cannot, against anyone's will, slip in among the masked ones on the freezing shelves at night. Moreover, his face worries, which their despairing ones could not. Moreover, sitting on an avocado crate "From the sun-kissed valleys of California," half in, half out of business, he sees us and nods, still sufficiently with it to eye with some interest Hattie's nearly empty shopping cart.

We go in. Or rather, since in is out, we step over, and I help Hattie draw her cart across the metal door runners that separate what is still, for a short time, the grocer's from the street.

All the thin-skinned fruits and vegetables—grapes, pears, tomatoes, lettuce—are gone from the store. Only the thick-skinned, semiperishable ones are left. I buy some oranges and then Hattie buys a little something from each crate. She touches each in farewell: "Five oranges, two of the two-for-forty-nine grapefruit; let me have four of the Idahos, please. . . ."

He goes expectantly from crate to crate with her, picking over, weighing in the tin basin of his clock-headed scale, thrusting into paper bags, his fingers making thick-spoked cages to transport fruit. He places the little rolled bags one by one in Hattie's shopping cart (he has run out of big bags). Then he looks away to the traffic commotion on the corner where a cement-mixing truck is easing its swollen, churning belly.

"Have you found another store yet?" Hattie asks him.

Looking away, he answers, "There's gonna be no store. There's no more place in New York for a poor man to buy a store. I'm gonna work for a chain."

He pounds his grimy, but thank God, fat fist on a bare, sloped bin. He draws in his breath and Hattie looks as if she is holding her breath as well. Slam, slam, slam goes the fist. We wait, expecting that now it will come pouring out. The hard work. The injustice. The indifference. But all the vegetable man says as he slams is, "Stamp, stamp, stamp! That's what I'll do all day, I'll stamp prices on the cans in the supermarket."

He follows us to his invisible demarcation, which separates what is still briefly his from the world. He looks toward the hollow concrete squares, like a prison for air, rising in air, on the corner.

"Some buildings they're putting up," he says appreciatively. "Strong, like for wartime."

On the walk back home, Hattie notices something and punches me on the arm to draw my attention. She sometimes does this and I'm sure she has no idea she does it—it's like the spontaneous, desperate clutch of a mute child.

Her punch draws my attention to the sign I had missed when I walked out this morning. Tacked to the wall of one of the still occupied brownstones: "On this site will be erected a 20-story luxury apartment house. . . ." I nod to show agreement with what I take the punch to signify —this is an indecency, like wrapping a shroud on a still living man to save undertaking time later.

The old lady sits out on a folding chair in front of the brownstone. She has always been there at the hour when the sun slants between two brownstones across the way.

Since the demolitions have begun, her schedule has changed, as if new solstices were occurring on the street.

She is a dry, brittle old lady, swathed in woolens even in springtime. One day—it was on another morning when Hattie had caught up with me in the street as she did today, and we had stopped to help the old lady pull her chair an inch or two over into the sunlight—the old lady astonished us both by telling us that she had a son, "a wonderful, huge big man." Without transition she went on, in a cracking, singing voice: "I took him out on the coldest days from morning till night, and when I got home I was blue in the face, but Lulie was nice and warm." It took us a moment to understand that we must squeeze this "huge big man" down to a baby again, as his mother did. After we had left the old lady, Hattie had asked me, "Where do you think Lulie is now? Where is the baby that is nice and warm?"

Over the old lady's head two X's have lately appeared, on the top floor.

"Will you move to Lulie's apartment?" Hattie asks now. Her popeyes brim with sympathy and show no awareness that she is giving the old lady a verbal punch.

The old lady stares while she takes all the seconds she needs to recover from the blow. "My son, Ludlow," she says—and the baby swells to giant proportions again— "lives in South America with his fourth wife. I'm moving to a home on West Seventy-fourth Street, just off Central Park West. The location's nice, except for the you-know-who moving in all around there."

"O—a home—that's—that's—" Hattie is spluttering, as if all the unexpressed sympathy and indignation on behalf of the laundryman and the vegetable man, all fermenting in a compost heap of daily trial watching, is struggling for expression. "I mean—I'm glad you feel you've settled it in your mind but still, still, for you, a home!"

The old lady clutches her pocketbook, which has been resting in her lap. It's a warning signal that she may be thinking of going.

"You'll still be a city dweller, then," I say. It's not that I feel the need to intercept Hattie's assault. But the old lady looks as if she may have a stroke.

"O I wouldn't leave the city!" the old lady says proudly, tremulously. "I love the gay life!"

"O! the way they go about doing things in this city!" Hattie wails. "It just forces everybody's hand. Disperse and dislocate! Before, storekeepers who made a poor living could get by, and people who were old and alone could manage, but now . . ."

"And I wouldn't live with children!" the old lady shouts. "I'm far too independent."

"Well, anyhow, you're not moving right away . . ." I say soothingly, falsely.

"That's right, I'm taking my time, don't you worry. They can't push me out. I've got a whole month . . ."

"And if there's anything we can do to help . . ."

"What about your house?" The old lady creaks her folding chair in the cold sunlight and turns sharply to Hattie. "They'll be pushing you out, too, never fear."

Hattie shakes her head slowly, sorry to disappoint. "No, the owners won't sell. Their married daughter has a cheap apartment there. And Miss Lamb's landlady lives in her house."

"They'll all sell when the offer goes high enough."

"We haven't heard anything about it."

"Do you realize—" the old lady is becoming excited again —"that a person who bought a building in the Depression, one of these old brownstones, say, for a few thousand dollars, can sell it now for a quarter of a million?"

"Yes, and look at the misery they inflict," says Hattie, "for that quarter of a million."

"What misery?" the old lady asks suspiciously. "What misery?"

Hattie's bugged and brimming eyes plainly spell out, You, look at you!

After a little suspicious interval the old lady's interest revives. "There's more going on in this street now than for the last fifteen years."

"I'm sorry you have to move," Hattie says with a sigh. "You must be feeling uprooted."

"You must be out of your mind," the old lady says promptly.

And although there is still a good ten minutes' sun, slanting through the broken walls of the former furnished rooms for single gentlemen only, the old lady rises, claps together her folding chair and then stands over it, fumbling for a grip on the wood with her arthritic claw.

"O *don't* go in just because I said that!" Hattie pleads.

She lets the handle of her cart fall with a clang and the little loosely rolled-up bags slip out, the grapefruits, oranges and Idahos rolling along the broken sidewalk.

I stoop to get them back inside the wagon. When I look up again, Hattie is mounting the steep, red-painted cement steps of the brownstone in pursuit of the old lady. She puts her hands on the old lady's chair.

"Please let me at least carry this."

The old lady lets go so abruptly and, it appears, viciously, that the chair falls clattering down the stone steps. Hattie must retrieve it in all her heavy clumsiness. By the time Hattie has opened the outer door and placed the chair in the hallway the old lady relents enough to say, "All right then. All right. You mean well, I suppose. Thank you."

"I'm so sorry if I said anything to offend you."

"Don't underestimate the people who are remaking this street," the old lady scolds, quite without heat, as if that had been the offense. "This street is going to be one of the finest, most exclusive streets in the whole city. You won't be able to touch an apartment under three hundred dollars a month. They'll have only the most exclusive tenants. I've been sitting and watching out there for months. I've seen the trend."

"Why do you approve?" Hattie asks desperately. "You won't be here!"

The old lady's chin begins to tremble as though she believes it possible that now Hattie will begin to speak of dying.

"I mean," Hattie says quickly, "they're forcing you out!"

"Thank you, dear." The old lady clutches the wooden back of her chair and drags it to a door at the back of the hall behind the stairway.

Hattie and I start again, without speaking, to walk through the din and dust of our street.

After a few steps, Hattie bursts out, "I know that was awful. I couldn't stop myself. The thought of her in a home —I know thousands of old ladies go into homes—but I've *seen* this one every day and the thought of her lying in a bed—'Matron, dear, could I have my bed a little closer to the window? Could I please have my heart pills, in that little box my Lulie gave me?' But I *should* have stopped myself."

We gaze, as we walk, at the primordial scene, complete with prehistoric monsters in the ooze and slime. The gigantic cranes that stretch their necks above, crashing their jaws; the mammoth trucks whose bellies revolve cement.

"Will you be coming later to watch, Jean?" It's Hattie's closing formality. Although I've gone every day now—for how long?—neither of us acknowledges that it might be taken for granted.

"I'll have to see how the work goes this afternoon. . . ."

"Of course. I'll call you to check, later. . . ."

She crosses the street to her own side, edging her belly past the cement mixer's belly, a procreator in a Procrustean city. . . .

On the short walk back to my own house, I stumble suddenly over broken pavement. The bloody woman, the digger through the rubble of last night's corpses, has nudged me again as I pick my way through the rubble of the street.

Seven |

At five, at exactly five (that's bullfighter, death-in-the-afternoon time, you told me) Hattie and I sit before the TV and we become a silent movie. We are the old Maya Deren, Cinema 16 silent movie. *Meshes* (Vincent liked art movies) *of the Afternoon.*

First there is the music. A dragging sound, like something in chains. That's meant to suggest the patriarch, the tables of the law. All that heaviness that once meant order, the discipline needed for survival. I ought to understand that.

The music takes on an ominous sound. Something rumbling from underneath.

A small-faced man narrates. His voice weak and light. An advertisement disguised as not an advertisement from a Jewish real-estate firm.

None of that seems to matter. I begin to sweat. My heart pounds. I glance secretively at Hattie. She is crouched over her swollen belly as if to protect it. Her pretty face contorts. The whole thing suggests premature labor pains.

We sit on hard kitchen chairs drawn up before the TV, watching. As if putting ourselves to school.

The eyewitnesses, their faces designed into masks, wrinkled, some of them, as water is wrinkled, all at once, by some gigantic force—the wind or the tidal pull of the moon. Their voices, in translation, disembodied.

There is something about Hattie's face that's unreal. There must be about my own, too. Something about the way we both move—or don't move—while we are watching.

Hattie and I are an experimental, silent film reacting to a film on TV. The old speeded-up, slowed-down, silent film. We fall endlessly, soundlessly from our chairs. We roll on the floor, we clutch our wombs. Soundless, endless groans.

Eight |

Another of my ordinary mornings. On my way from my desk—where I've been writing my two paragraphs—to the kitchenette to make breakfast. A mauve envelope under my door.

I pick it up and put it unopened on my eating table. I can always wait to read a letter. Sometimes I can even wait when the letter's from you.

In this case I pretty much know what's in this letter. I already know it must be from Sostana, one flight up. Probably it is about her son, Mario.

I remember what you said about Sostana. It will do for a paragraph one morning. *Loftus says that Sostana gives the impression of having mismanaged her life. But that she is probably one of those people to whom life has genuinely presented impossible alternatives.*

I suppose she is seven or eight years older than I. She and I have discussed many painful things, but needless to say we've never discussed age. Here her life has set her down, a no longer quite so handsome Italian woman, who's ended up in New York with little money, no husband and a nonfunctioning son.

I have already considered that it might have been Mario's nightmare that woke me again last night after all, not my own. Mario is twelve, but a hefty boy. Mario thumps the floor with his feet and Sostana shrieks once or twice. She says she wishes she had the self-control to keep silent, but she shrieks in spite of herself. Mario gets up and hurls himself, eyes open but fast asleep, at the furniture. Sostana shrieks whenever she thinks he has hurt himself. He is a big, husky boy, and too strong for her. The duet subsides only when he exhausts himself. Then she walks him back to bed. Last night my nightmare coincided with Mario's just as Jesús' did that first night.

For a moment when I woke last night, but very faintly, my body remembered those five thumps of Jesús. The lover knocks at the door on one side, the baby answers on the other. Jesús' thumps have dwindled to the tiny agitation a baby's fist might make. (And it is not many nights since his first visit.) "Women's bodies can absorb anything." That's a line from one of Hattie's recent manuscripts. "I feel my belly has engulfed a world." Sword swallowers and fire-eaters all.

Sostana's note, when I finally get to it. "Forgive all our dreadful pounding last night. I hope somehow we did not wake you, but I know that is not likely. It was only my poor son with his nightmares again. Fortunately they do not last long. But alas, they do not stop, either. . . ."

Reading it is somehow a relief that brings with it a strong temptation to crawl back into bed.

Therefore I stand up quickly and dress to go out. Slacks and sweater. Right thumb has India ink under the nail. No make-up, hair pulled back and fastened behind the ears with too many bobby pins. All that a reminder not to dawdle. Go out on the errand, then hurry home, where the work is.

A newly lettered sign is tacked above my desk: DO NOT TURN NIGHT INTO DAY.

Last night, just after Mario's nightmare it must have been, I woke in the dark again. My apartment, the whole brownstone, was silent. Despite the springtime smell that blew in through the open window, despite the lone drunk who sang cheerfully in the distance, something frightful had just been shoved behind a door.

I walk, at such times, snapping lights, to my desk. It is 3:00 A.M. or 4:00 A.M. "The dead of night," I say loudly. Only parody is useful. It is the equivalent of Sostana's shriek. "Don't get overdramatic," I say. "The dead of day also."

I begin to violate my disciplines, one by one. I stand at my worktable and begin to move things around. The manuscript of a chemistry textbook, seven hundred and fifty pages, the heavy book of type-face samples, my Haber-rule book . . .

Again I have the feeling my life is like a melodramatic portion of a shaky novel. ". . . *It was while she was sharpening a pencil, then testing its point on the ball of her index finger, that she at last saw the woman. Naked, at the bottom of a pit, covered with blood, clawing her way upward through corpses.*"

Hattie and I have extracted our private symbols of horror from the welter of horror symbols. Hattie has her pregnant women, her children, her Muslims. I have the woman who digs her half-dead way up through corpses.

order vs. despair

I sat to work. Any time I stopped I saw the woman. She was there all night, clawing her way. And all night I sat with my T-square and crow-quill pen and ink and onion-skin tissues. Lettering and laying out and bestowing order.

At 5:00 A.M. I can stop work. The digger was too exhausted for more. Before I went to bed I wrote, on the reverse of my sign that said DO NOT TURN NIGHT INTO DAY: "There is no one to turn it back for you."

In the morning at the sound of the alarm set for the usual time I crept from my bed and made once more for my desk. I opened my loose-leaf journal, bent over it as if it were a holy book. *Loftus says* . . . Loftus says what? I couldn't think what Loftus says. He says Erna is visiting him. Never mind that. Write *Loftus says* . . . A new fragment of the nightmare came back. No.

Loftus says that Freud says the pleasure principle is in conflict with the world.

Loftus says that Adler says what we remember determines the soul's development. Or is that turned around? And is it just the same reversed?

Loftus says that Jung says touching evil brings the danger of—I forget the word—is it succumbing to evil? Therefore don't succumb to anything. Don't even succumb to good. Is that enough to live on?

More of the nightmare came back. But the pen hand took over and lettered severely, STOP NOW.

"Darling Loftus—
"I've been writing down your wisdoms. The name of what I write down is called *Loftus says.* If Loftus says hands on hips then I do it. If Loftus doesn't say it then I don't. Do you see? But, darling, you said something that

56

Jung says and I want to talk to you about it. (If just Jung said it, and you didn't say he said it, then it wouldn't exist for me. What do I care about the zillions of books that have been written? It's got to come to me through you. Do you see that? But now I've found a book and I want to tell you about it so you can tell it back to me. Does that make sense?)

"There is this writer who died about five years ago and now a publisher is bringing out a collection of his magazine pieces. They asked me to design the book but I won't be able to do it—my desk is piled with stuff. Yesterday I was looking through the essays and something jumped out of the page. Because that morning I had been writing down, *Loftus says that Jung says don't succumb to good any more than to evil.*

"And then I was staring at it and thinking, yes, that's right, that's the way it's got to be now, but feeling so *empty.* And I thought, if he doesn't tell us something else we can feel about this knowledge of evil besides 'don't succumb to good either,' then how does he expect us to live through what we've already lived through and still have to go on living through? Because between those who were there and those who dreamed they were there we've been through everything, haven't we? Between the survivors and the ones who didn't survive we know it all. And after so much just this: don't succumb to anything, not even to good?

" 'The death of our old culture came about when the evil greater than evil occurred—which is the terror.' That's what this writer, Isaac Rosenfeld, who died and the publisher is reviving him now, said. And he said that because we have to live with the knowledge of evil greater than

57

evil, we also have to find a good greater than good. And he says that that good greater than good ought to be joy.

"'Terror beyond evil and joy beyond good: that is all there is to work with. . . . May the knowledge of joy come,' he said, 'and the knowledge of terror never leave!'

"I can't tell you what a feeling it gave me to read that. It was like a completion of the thought in what you said Jung said. A *translation* of the thought into another mode. For the ones who can't walk a tightrope of the mind. Like me. When I'm hoping there'll be some way of plunging in, heart, soul, and body again. Some bearable, honorable way.

"'What will we have to take joy in?' this man wrote. 'Our joy will be in love and restoration, in the sensing of humanity as the concrete thing. . . .'

"Tell me what you think, Loftus. 'May the knowledge of terror never leave!' He said that, too. Write me back about what this man says. Write me, darling. . . ."

Nine |

Inside my brownstone, cool and dark, people are standing before their open doors as if drilling for disaster.

I have been conscious all morning that it is Friday, Loftusday. I forgot it was the once-a-month Friday, the exterminator's day.

The exterminator is a jolly young fellow with wife and child in Hicksville. He squirts the juice from his gun with real satisfaction. "That'll get 'em." The streams are milky, like jets from a cow's udder. All of us who are home at that hour are drawn into the hall to escape the fumes. Mrs. Jensco stands with her clipboard checking off apartments.

Edgar, the homosexual on the top floor, a very correct and discreet one, who manages an art movie theater, calls from the stairway above, "I saw some silverfish in my tub last night."

"This'll take care of silverfish, too," says our exterminator.

"I feel like an informer," Edgar says. "I kind of like silverfish, after all."

59

Sostana is standing quietly in her doorway. She is apparently going in late to work today because of last night's nightmares. Next to her is a new young man. A homosexual of the soppier kind, anxious to curry some favor out of Edgar's dignity. "I know what you mean," he says excitedly. "It's sort of like telling the police where Anne Frank is hiding."

Edgar receives this shocking remark in silence. But the new young man blunders on, eager to strike some chord that will seduce Edgar's dignified attention.

He hits on everybody's daily reading matter, the trial. "Don't you feel," he throws up the stairwell desperately, "the more you read, that you tend to classify the people you know according to those horrible types? I mean like I find myself thinking, so-and-so is a gold-tooth salvager. He wouldn't actually kill any Jews, but like he'd inform on them to get their apartment?"

Edgar's dignity is unmoved.

It is Mrs. Jensco who says severely, "No silverfish in this house, thank you."

Our house is very clean. The apartments, eleven of them, including the owner's apartment in the basement, are free of roaches. The smell lasts all through Friday night. An unmistakable, layered smell. A coated sweetness that seems to puncture itself at intervals to get at the gagging poison.

By the time you came to see me on Fridays I'd gotten used to the smell. From the way you stood at my doorway, drawing sharp breaths I could tell the smell was strongly there. You're sensitive to smells. Erna, you told me once, smelled of cigarettes and self-pity. Because Erna smoked, I didn't. I made strong coffee in the percolator on Friday nights and I wore perfume. I didn't pity myself at all on Fridays.

The exterminator starts inexorably to the stairs.

"O spare his silverfish," the soppy fairy says, still trying.

Mrs. Jensco says to him with surprise, "Didn't you read your *Trib* yesterday?"

"I did read it," he says doubtfully. "I'm sure I read it."

"Well, you must have missed the article I mean. Didn't you read it?"—she turns to Sostana—"Actually, a pack of rats was seen running along the street uptown from a demolition on Delancy Street?"

Sostana answers from her doorway in her fined-down Italian accent, "Poor rats. Where should they go, eh? They are dispossessed."

Mrs. Jensco, as if to assure herself, nods at Sostana's door. The exterminator edges himself and his equipment amiably in. "Excuse me while I dispossess some things in here."

In spite of the little fusses we make on once-a-month Fridays, we are glad to be here, glad to be in a clean building, temporarily safe amid the encroaching wrecks and disasters of the city.

Sometimes, in an apartment house, doors stay shut for months. You see no one coming and no one going. The sounds you occasionally hear from the neighbors' apartments are made by voices in the television programs they are tuned to. Your neighbors recede from you. You are as alone as in frontier days, surrounded by acres of wooded land and barbed wire at the outposts. But once in a while the doors blow open, and then it is hard to shut them again.

As the exterminator leaves my apartment, Sostana walks in.

"I want to apologize," she says, "for those terrible noises last night. You must have heard them."

I have already read her note, so I don't bother pretending not to know what she means.

"I didn't come upstairs," I say, "because I know you want to handle it alone."

"You are right," she says bitterly. "I handle everything alone."

My work is spread on my desk. I am longing to get at it. It's one of the things I do on Friday to affect the smells in my apartment. After a hard, concentrated day I can take a simple view of myself and my life. My own smells then, I feel, are less layered, less dense. Once you sniff past the exterminator's leavings you get a sharp, clear sense impression of me as you like me best.

"I say to him," Sostana goes on, " 'Please, darling, mummy is here, there is nothing to be afraid of.' That is how I lie to him, that is how I handle it. That is the story of all my life—I handle it with a lie."

Sostana's story, a bitter one, I already know. It unravels itself into the silent, bitter-smelling room while I pour out coffee for us.

The story starts with her first name and ends with her last.

"My name is Sostana!" she says, with her cultivated Italian's accent. "It means sustained, eh!" She gives her bitter laugh. "Wherever I go everything is falling apart."

Her family name, in Italy, was Duecastile. She has shown me her crest. They owned, at one time, two castles. "But what good was it? A useless name. Useless castles, no more money, nothing but one old house with old valueless things in it. During the war and after the war, when the American soldiers were there, my eyes opened. I wanted to be free of that name. I did not want to live the useless life that my useless name forced upon all my family. I fell in love with Peter . . ." She stops, she seems stunned by what she has said.

"What do you think, Jean?" she continues. "When you don't love someone any more it is impossible to believe you ever did, eh?"

I move restlessly among my things when she says that. It is the kind of talk that leaves bitter odors in the apartment.

Sostana goes on. "So we married. We came to America. What happiness, eh! A new name, a new life. And then, God, the suffering. And the divorce, what a relief! And then again I see it. I am a woman with a meaningless name. Mrs. Lampert. Who is that? There is already a new Mrs. Lampert. The old one is erased. I am a woman of obscurity who has not even any more her own name, which was already meaningless when I was born. My poor son cannot get from one end of the night to the other without a nightmare to ride upon. I cannot get through the day without one."

I move around uneasily.

"I am like the rats who are running from a demolition, eh? From one ruined building to another. Where is my life to take shelter? How can I give shelter to my son when I have none?"

Very soon I am going to say firmly that I really must work.

"You will find something," I murmur over my coffee cup.

But Sostana says no. "What I think is that I have been given a meaningless life to live."

After a while, Sostana says, "How lucky you are to have your work. Something that really has meaning for you." Because of her accent, Sostana has been able to find a saleslady's job in a snooty Fifth Avenue leather-goods store.

I look at my desk protectively. I feel like a mother who says, to avoid the evil eye, "My daughters aren't *really* pretty."

"My work doesn't take care of everything," I say. I think of last night. How my work saved me from drowning. I can't allow myself such disloyalty, so now I admit, "That's the nature of the work. Even a bad book, one that misses its own meaning, has an intention. The designer coaxes out the intention. He drops the useless parts and makes, by his own desire for meaning, a meaning—at least a visual meaning."

Now I want to be protective of my work again. I am sorry to have revealed so much to someone whose envy and bitterness spring up so readily.

Sostana pursues me. "And what if the book is about— no meaning?"

"Why, then," I say lightly, "I suppose what I do is give it style. Beautiful margins and good type and headbands and illustrated end papers, if the budget allows."

"You give it a funeral casket." Sostana smiles at my beautiful daughter, wishing it harm.

"I don't feel that way about it," I say angrily.

Sostana changes the subject at once. "How are the foursome?"

I am startled. Have I told her—and how much? Apparently I have. I'd forgotten, in fact, that she had been here once for dinner with the foursome.

"They are still the foursome." I nod and shrug.

"They walk in their sleep, those four!" Sostana is bitter again. "They hold each other's hands. They take a sip of coffee, put down their coffee cups and take each other's hands. If one of them ever woke up, that foursome would break open like a soap bubble. Hattie will be the one to break into the smallest pieces. *Dio!* Don't I remember how a woman falls into a stupor when she is pregnant. After the happy dream there is the nightmare."

I think of Hattie crouched over her belly, watching the trial. The happy dream?

"You wait, when her child is born, that will be an end to the foursome."

The poisons in my apartment are beginning to make me feel sick. The exterminator's spray mingled with Sostana's bitter streams. Jet after jet of woman's milk turned lethal.

Sostana suddenly jumps up from her chair to go.

"Don't be angry!" She gives me a disarming foreign woman's glance—amused and sad. "Whatever I say— please. Today I am dull and stupid. We had such a bad night, my poor Mario and I."

How charmingly a foreign woman knows how to complain. Sostana has managed, by hard effort, to recapture the tone of herself—the design, the style of a civilized woman. She leaves, in the apartment, a patina of sad, worldly charm.

The moment she is gone, I take my jar of marigolds to the window sill of the window you always look up at before you enter the building.

I work without looking at the clock or stopping for

lunch. When I feel I am finished, ready to put my pencils away, I glance at the time. It is after four thirty. In a few minutes, the phone rings.

But it is not Hattie. It's you. O my dear. . . .

"Were you just going out? Did I just catch you?"

You are breathless, you are sad.

"What is it? Why aren't you on the train?"

"Erna sent a wire. She's coming. She begs that we settle this in person. It's too important for letters, she says. What can I do? There was no time even to wire her back no."

"She's coming." I am about to say, O what's so terrible about that? But I have wailed it out a second time, "Coming!"

Visions of Erna. Erna, the too-hastily buried woman in the House of Usher, rising up through her coffin nails; Erna as Medea, bringing her gift of psychological understanding that will burn away Loftus' flesh. . . . (Why doesn't she come to see me instead, the coward?)

"It seems so unreal. Friday afternoon and I'm not rushing to catch the train to come to you. Instead I'm waiting for her. I dread it . . ."

"Loftus . . . darling . . . listen . . ."

"I have a terrible urge to run for the train, anyway. But I can't just run away, can I?"

Hold my breath. Then, "Of course not."

"We've had children together. I have to remind myself of that. Now they're grown they seem no part of her or me, except by my loving them. I had to remind myself . . ."

"Will she fall into your arms, you think, after all this time?"

"God, no!" He sounds horrified.

"Hold me in your arms instead . . . in spirit . . ."

"I will. I do. O my dear. . . ."

As soon as we hang up there comes the ring that's been waiting, lurking along the wire. Hattie's call. To say she's been trying to get me, and now it's 4:45.

When you come on Fridays one of the first things you do is walk to the worktable and look at the work. I leave it spread out for you to look at. You appreciate it now like an *aficionado*. In calligraphy you know good from bad. When it comes to machine-set type you know the fine stuff, too. I taught you to look first at the g's and e's. After you've looked at everything, you carefully put all the tissues together. Close the type book, put my pencils back in the Dundee marmalade jar (beautifully black on white) and say softly and seriously, "Put it away now, love. Put it all away."

Today is Friday. Here (somewhere) is your letter, saying plainly you won't come. All the same you come, like someone newly dead, to appear where you have always appeared. You stand at my table. You bend over it. Who is that shrieking? "Don't touch my work!"

It's Friday and you lean over my desk again. "It's time to close the book now, love . . ."

Erna speeds toward you on the train.

"Don't touch my work . . . !"

Ten |

How can any grief compare with this grief?

I don't listen.

I don't watch, either, although my eyes, like Hattie's, see the close-up of the woman's face on the TV screen.

Hattie drinks in the words. Hattie sucks up the images. This is watching TV as TV means to be watched, as children watch. Her shoulders watch, her knees watch. Her fetus thrusts forward to watch. A TV cartoon animator would show the fetus slipping out, all pale and amniotized, to get a better look at the screen, then slipping back again. It doesn't happen. Hattie still bears the fetus that bears witness to the witness on TV who is bearing witness at the trial.

This woman's face, close up on TV, is calm, even normal. Not unusually lined. It is her voice that is somehow faded, wrinkled. It floats in, from time to time, from somewhere off the TV screen, a shadow behind the translator's crisp words.

The witness is speaking of killings. She remarks, as if

unable to help herself, ". . . And I remember . . . it was such a beautiful, clear October morning. . . ."

I don't listen. I had from the first day made up my mind not to listen. I am in this not for me or for them or for Hattie. I am in it for you.

Every day, somehow, at quarter to five my type books close, my layout sheets are gathered under the *millefleurs* glass paperweight you gave me for my birthday.

This holy ritual at five began merely because my lover asked me to keep an eye on his former student. I long to be indispensable to my lover and to his concerns. I must be, if I am to win.

My mind sleeps. My bones, my sly, self-pitying bones, creep off to the past.

I jerk them back. I don't want them there, either.

Creep, creep, they keep creeping off. Throw on a sheet and clanking chain. "I am the spirit of October past."

October Morn at college. The mice mazes. The pictures John Oates, my psychology professor, mentor, and lover showed me. The wonder of the world.

"S—s—s—" Hattie gasps. God! Giving birth? No. Only listening and watching her TV program. The child with the child inside.

Creep off to myself then as I was at that time, at that moment. In the same woman's college where Loftus now teaches, but didn't then, and where I was once, an age ago, a student. I meet myself there, intact. I know my life developed from that point, but it feels as if that time of my life sits in a frame. Picturesque, brilliantly lit or gloomily dark.

It is "October Morn." Only a woman's college could

tolerate such a delicately snickering joke. Chapel bells clang, students hurry along the paths, clasping their brown bags of lunch, and making frantic efforts to reach their friends in time to start on the hike up the mountain. At the end of one path looms a Gothic pile of stones. At the turreted top is the Psych Lab. The Lab is dark till the lights go on.

(I have again a sense of encountering my life in a novel I dislike—so unbalanced—long empty stretches, then suddenly overdramatic.)

The figures hurrying along the path begin, as if to capture my attention, to jog up and down. They enlarge and stiffen themselves like pop ups in a children's book. O the dear little cardboard figures!

Here is dear little Jeannie on the path, too. Hold the tab and push her along.

She is going to the Psych Lab. She is supposed to help feed the mice, but now that the bells are announcing October Morn, she is not sure whether Professor Oates will be there. She carries two lunch bags, just in case.

She reaches the second landing of the wooden stairway (see the dear little pop-up mice in their electrified cages) and hears a voice. Professor Oates is listening to the radio. The announcer of a local station is describing the events of October Morn just as they are at that moment taking place.

". . . On bright October Morn the air is like a crisp apple. No one knows just when the bell will ring. One moment it is an ordinary morning before classes begin, and the next moment the bell begins its loud, clanging summons. The cooks have had to know all along. They have the cold pails of egg salad, piles of sliced cheese. The students make their sandwiches, tuck in an apple or a bunch of grapes, stuff it all into a paper bag and are off, wearing the time-honored old cut-down jeans and men's shirts, off to climb Mount Ellena. . . ."

A bit of static and then the announcer continues heartily: "It's a fine, healthy tradition up at the college. And so, if you wondered what the loud bell-ringing was about this morning, you know that it was the beginning of the yearly celebration of October Morn, the climb up to Mount Ellena for the young women up at St. Alban's College. . . ."

See the dear little mice in their electrified cages? Professor John Oates is feeding them. They squeak. But whether in pleasure or confusion, Jeannie doesn't know. He is deconditioning them. Each mouse has been striking a lever and winning its pellet all summer long. Now it is time for the new students in the lab to recondition the mice.

Through the mullioned windows, on the path, see the dear little groups of girls. They are calling to their friends. And singing, "A woman never knows what a good man she's got until she turns him down. . . ."

"Innocence," Professor Oates says to Jeannie, when she comes in. "Freezing innocence."

(See the dear professor. How tall and skinny and anxious he is. See how he pops up when Jeannie comes in.)

The top floor of the psychology building is musty. Everything gives off darkness—the varnish of the long brown tables, the mice mazes, the electrified cages where a mouse receives a pellet for a right move, a shock for a wrong one. Every semester, for three credits, the mice are put through their paces, or mazes. The girls in Professor Oates' classes feel awe for the learning capacity of the mouse and, by extension, for man.

Jeannie has, like them, written into her notebook her teacher's words: "What behavioral attitudes might man not master, given the proper training?"

Red-eyed John Oates glares. (See the dear red eyes.)

"Why aren't you out there having fun?"

The professor rushes from cage to cage, frightening the animals. Then he stops and asks if Jeannie hears anything. She hears the singing outdoors. No, in the room, he says. The mice squeaking? No, not the mice. Then she hears how the sinks run a rusty, hissing song.

Professor Oates tells her that that sound gets into his dreams at night. A combination, he says, of the Saturday horror serials of his boyhood—the monster scientist about to cut up his victim and pointing out with an evil laugh that all the blood will go down the drain—and the reality of now. All this is happening now, he tells her. Happening! In 1944! Has been going on for years and still is, in the midst of war. An Army psychologist friend has shown him photographs taken by the military and has described other captured pictures. Experimental cell blocks, drains in the tiled floors, all that. It hardly matters that these are Germans, Professor Oates says. What matters is that men have done it. Men like himself—teachers, students, lovers of science. They have replaced the mice in the maze with men.

"So that all men shall stand amazed," John Oates says softly. He looks young and ill and frightened. Absent-mindedly, he squashes a bread pellet in his fingers.

72

The bells toll only now and then. Through the dormer windows a glimpse of dazzling day.

John Oates puts on the table for Jeannie to see a photograph of a scene that is destined to become one of the classic sights of the world (see the dear professor about to seduce the virgin) like Stonehenge, like the Parthenon in moonlight, like the ruined cities of Angkor Wat, like the Great Pyramid at Giza—the piled-up stick bodies at the bottom of a lime pit.

(Do not try to pop up the bodies in the lime pit.)

Jeannie's soul is fainting. (Don't be afraid of such language, go on and use it, especially in a pop up.) She is about to enter one of those long larval sleeps that mark the end of a lived-out phase.

(Make the girl's pop up go down again, while she says, "I can't bear it.")

She sinks with John Oates to the floor, in her boy's shirt and jeans, riveted fly and all, beneath the mice maze.

"My harvest fruit," John Oates murmurs. "Without a blemish on your apple body. Only joy can cancel out that horror."

(See the dear couple. Take the tab and waggle them back and forth.)

Professor Oates, the behaviorist, feels remorse. "I seduced you with dirty pictures. An orphan. A Dean's List girl."

Jeannie is not sorry. She feels no connection with her classmates, singing on the mountain.

"I hope you won't hate me," John Oates says. "My darling girl, I hope you won't."

She shakes her head. Never. She is passionately for the

breakdown of her life. "A catastrophe has changed the world. The old forms have no more meaning for me. I will never marry or have children."

"All the same," he says sadly, "you'd be surprised how life goes on. Even I know that. . . ."

One day it came to pass that she did hate him. Her soul had fainted and the singing world had fallen down a mountain and she had lain beneath mice mazes with her teacher. But nothing had changed. John Oates still lived with his wife and daughter. He and Jeannie still lay down together, when they could, beneath the mice mazes. The war in Europe was over but the war with Japan continued. Europe's death camps had been come upon, one by one, like monsters' lairs, full of stinking bones. The president of the college, at convocation, spoke of "these troubled times." Nobody ran around like those open-mouthed faces she later saw in Picasso's "Guernica," with pointed, screaming tongues. The girls still calmly brushed their Stroock tweed skirts and cold-water-washed their cashmeres.

She asked herself what had happened. The world shook. Was she the only one who fell down?

It was by now near the end of her junior year. She was of course a psychology major. She sat at the back of every one of John Oates' lectures. He enjoyed lecturing. He knew himself, he told them, for a Sheldon cerebretonic type—probably a four-four-seven—weak on muscle and nerve control, and no Epicurean, strong on thinking. Tall, lanky, nervous, he paced back and forth, his tie swinging.

He posed for the class a riddle to which Jeannie, the privileged disciple, had already been given the answer.

"It's tricky, and requires flexibility of approach. Don't let your minds close down too tightly over the problem:

What is the relationship among these numbers—34-42-50-59-66-72?"

Long, baffled silence while the students scribbled out geometric progressions that didn't work.

Then a voice from the back of the room: "The stops on the West Side IRT Subway in Manhattan."

John Oates is stone-still. He does not even look in Jean's direction. His light-washed spectacles glint with shock. In her fright it seems to Jean that the spectacles shatter. Shards of glass pierce her flesh.

"S-s-s!" Hattie sucks in through her teeth. Cradles her belly. The program is over. Neither of us can manage to stand up to turn off the TV. We are both waiting for images to recede into the background.

There's always some evasiveness, possibly shame, in that first look we give each other after the program.

"Don't go," Hattie says, looking over her shoulder toward the kitchen in an absent-minded way. "Let's have a cup of tea or a drink or anything." Then she looks quickly back in my direction and says doubtfully, "I know you like to be home early on Friday, though."

I acknowledge coolly that you can't make it. I betray nothing, Loftus.

"O then stay!" She blushes. In spite of the chapters of her life she sends me in the mail each week, she is shy with me. And in awe, too, and determined not to let the awe matter.

I am glad to accept. Her sister and brother-in-law are coming, too, so I will be ring-around-a-rosy'd by the foursome. I am afraid to sit out the evening alone in still another movie, hearing the imagined conversation of you and lawful wife Erna through newsreel, comedy, love scene. And not knowing, finally, which might be which. *I thought you didn't care, that was why I left. O no. I thought you were the one who didn't care, that was why I didn't beg you to come back. . . .*

Hattie gets up, wobbling, to go to the kitchen. I am trying to summon back my bones so that I can get up for a cigarette.

My bones take their time about creeping back. They come by way of the reunion two years ago. Why does anyone go to a reunion at a college they hated, for the first time after fifteen years? God knows. To prove it's no longer dangerous. To prove the tricky riddle has a solution outside the mind-set.

I had left school right after the incident of the false geometric progression. I had money from my aunt, my sole remaining relative. I had written her that if she ever intended to give me any money it should be now. I was very fierce with her and probably she thought I was pregnant. But after a few attempts, she gave up trying to ask questions and sent me the money.

I went to New York, lived in a girl's residence, took my first job as a Girl Friday in a printing shop, learned printing during the day and design at night and rode those subway stations (34-42-50-59-66-72) with a sense of betrayed and betraying every time.

A quick plunge into an affair, anyone handy—the owner of the print shop—to take away the burning sensation of the last. From that one to easy others. Making sure the man is married. Another reason for going to the reunion. It came at the end of the off-and-on three-year affair with Vincent.

There are only two things to add to what you already know about Vincent. First, he was, of course, married. This kept me secure for a long time; I never had to reconsider my vow. And secondly, he had been in Germany, had actually been in on the liberating of a concentration camp. He wooed me, you might say, with that, though he didn't know it. It scared me then. I wondered myself if I might finally have gone berserk on pain. If all that excruciated feeling had broken through the dividing line and become sex. Not so. But in those days it was still true that if someone said "concentration camp" to me, my body and soul emptied out. I was ready to faint, to fall down. I marveled at anyone who remained standing. In those days there were only two kinds of people for me—those who knew and those who didn't know. And it had nothing to do with reading newspapers.

Then the reunion. My former roommate, who had stayed aloofly puzzled through junior year, passed through from Cleveland expressly to pick me up in her car. Good-fellowship and curiosity. Plump. Mother of four.

"We're thirty-four years old, Jeannie, can you believe it? Let's go back and see what's become of all those others. You really made it in New York. The rest of us who stayed and got degrees have nothing to show but our loosened girdles. . . ."

Good-fellowship and flattery. "What really happened, Jeannie? After all these years, tell . . . ?"

My class, the class of '46, paraded in blond wigs and long beads and carried fluffy parasols on which was lettered, "No time for frivolity in '46's 4 years."

I felt a combined nausea and glee at all this, pretending to share history with them. But I knew their history slipped smoothly back around a pleasant curve, while mine dropped off the edge of the world.

My classmates and I reminded each other that our four years included ration books, knitting for Russian War Relief, cleaning our own rooms, asking soldiers to dance in the town USO, going to the Veterans' Hospital and reading to the boys with green tags pinned to their bathrobes —the psychological cases; that we had helped to harvest apples on manless farms near school, that we had been in school when Roosevelt died, and some of those who "accelerated" were also there in the summer when the bells clanged for VJ Day. And before, when the concentration camps were liberated and U.S. soldiers carried out the stick bodies, two and three to an armful.

One year after I left school, after John Oates had shown me the photographs, all that secret horror he had whispered to me that October Morn was generally known. The local newsreel theaters showed the released Army films. If John Oates hadn't told me then, I had wondered, sitting and drinking sherry with my cheerful former classmates, if I had found out, along with everyone else, would it have seemed less like my own personal catastrophe?

Another reason for going to the reunion. I would soon be an old priest. Thirty-five, thirty-six, thirty-seven, thirty-eight . . . It was the false progression I was wrestling with. Forty, forty-one, forty-what? I would be past the age of sacrifice, of choosing not to have children. When I was past childbearing, what then? Would I still let myself believe that the terribleness of the times had led me to renounce children? There would be no more choice. Whether I married or not would then be of no interest. What bitterness would I live for then?

I had wandered back, for old times' grief, to the Psychology Lab. The mice were still squeaking. But they were no longer the same mice. The man tending them was also not the same.

A medium height, somewhat stocky man. With a different, more physical, less nervous kind of energy. A not unattractive man. Former Psychology Professer Oates might have classed present Psychology Professor Genarian as *Loftus* predominantly somatatonic, with even a bit of viscerotonic thrown in. A reflective, gentle, even somewhat sad-looking man. I thought to myself, a Jew. But as it turned out, you were not.

"I used to be the student assistant to the man who was head of the Psychology Department then," I say. My smile is rueful. Looking back on the past from new and worldly eminences.

"And are you working now in science?" Your tone cordial, even (did you know?) a trifle fatherly, *in loco* the previous head of the department.

"O no, I'm down on science," I say, laughing. "Early trauma," I add, laughing. "I'm in graphics now. I freelance a good many books on science, though."

That strikes you as highly interesting. You are, as a matter of fact, working on a textbook yourself. It would be good to have someone designing it who knows the subject. May you mention my name to your publisher?

"O yes, I've done a good deal of work with the art editor there."

"Have you? Isn't that fine, then it might work out very well, mightn't it? I enjoy getting to New York whenever I can. A bachelor's life at a girl's college—" You grin, and I grin back; we share a pleasant complicity of lechery, because I am a New York woman and you want it understood you are no hayseed, this bucolic setting notwithstanding—"can be limiting."

(It didn't take me long to learn from my fellow '46'ers —I, who had picked my secretive way among them, could now give and receive information—what you had concealed: a wife from whom you were separated, a rumored affair with a teacher at the college. These concealments pleased me.)

I stand before the mice mazes, helping you feed the mice. My feet on the very spot. We smile at each other, already liking each other well enough to deceive. I am coming to the decision that I will not be an old priest. I have not been a student of Pavlov's for nothing. I will decondition myself from shock. When the bell rings I will salivate and I will be fed.

I had wanted to know if I could see myself in those other women of my time. But then I couldn't see myself in them when I went back. I didn't begin to see myself in anybody else until I met Hattie.

Eleven |

If you think of the foursome the way Sostana does, like children holding hands in a perpetual ring-around-a-rosy, then Hattie is the one who falls down prematurely, as the children come to "Ashes, Ashes," and is pulled to her feet so she can fall at the proper time.

But what I think when I visit the foursome is that the four of them together make a room. Each is a wall that leans on the others, depending on them for its continuation. It needs them to round its own corners, to come into balance with itself, to enter into the state of room.

A wall cemented to other walls is immovable, a room. On the other hand, what freedom! They say what they like to each other, what they need to say. Sometimes it's like a session in group therapy. Sitting in close, the better to bite. But also they use each other for their self-improvement, a system of checks and balances against which to measure themselves.

There is freedom and smugness in their closeness. (I suppose it's that which insults and enrages Sostana in her loneliness.) They have assigned personalities and roles to themselves in order to enjoy their foursome to the fullest. As if the four humors have been parceled out among them so that they, in their cosiness, might represent the varieties of the universe.

Hattie is judged to be inclined to melancholy—idealistic, naïve, hence quick to judge, hence prone to disappointments and hectic proposals for reform. Ezra is choleric—selfish and gifted, an artist and, with his quickness of response, a potential philanderer. Lillian is sanguine—overprotective and sentimental, loving and foolish, and sustaining. Stanwood is steady. It's phlegm, they suppose, that keeps him balanced, like a sack of sand in the trunk of a car on an icy road.

These are only their public roles, however. Public, that is, to the foursome. They all, as I learn from Hattie's letters, guard secret personalities.

They come in one by one, the members that complete the foursome. Ezra, lean and nervous, unloading his cameras and pouches from his shoulders; Lillian pretty and flushed; Stanwood pudgy and tired-looking.

"Jean, how grand you're staying!" Lillian kisses me on the cheek. Ezra and Stanwood greet me with a kind of affectionate relief—the reliable neighbor who watches with Hattie.

After dinner the three walls, Ezra, Stanwood, Lillian, take their time about looking at fourth-wall Hattie. They examine at leisure her chips, cracks, bulges. They thump for wall faults.

"You really are being too self-centered about this," Stanwood says. "All this pain wasn't suddenly invented, now, to make you personally suffer. It was always there, Hattie, even before TV."

"A little distance, Hattie," Ezra says. "A little perspective."

"Hattie is too sensitive, anyway, to be watching," says Lillian. "Not to mention her condition."

The three nod with satisfaction at Hattie. They have pried loose another rotten flake.

Lillian's comment, the most lovingly said, interests Hattie the least. At the moment she prefers the two male walls, the thumpers. She turns her face to them.

Tonight Hattie has about her all the classic signs of romantic intenseness. A slender, hollow-cheeked look, dark hair. She is really very fair-skinned, as fair as her blond sister, Lillian. But whereas with Lillian the fairness has a pink, Rubens tinge, as if she were about to be buxom but decided on second thought rather not, with Hattie it is pallor. In reality, her hair is a pale brown, her eyes of the same watery color, the eyelids looking pink-tinged, either from weeping or eyestrain. An indistinct, seemingly featureless face. She is a Van Eyck—very narrow in her limbs and joints, very swollen in her pregnancy. Lillian has already whispered tearfully to me that the doctor has said Hattie will have difficulty even with a normal delivery, that if there are any complications . . .

Hattie protests back to the thumper walls. "I mean when we pass on the human race what are we passing on? Do we know? Can we trust it? Are we monsters, passing on monstrous traits to more monsters to whom we teach a few surface manners the way they teach apes to ride bicycles? A few moral concepts that sit like tiny hats on top of our swollen, horror-filled heads?"

"O Hattie," Lillian moans.

"What I can't stand is that I'm twenty-four and I'm an

expert on torture. That's the fantastic thing. They're making me into an expert on torture."

Stanwood picks up his chair, moves it around the table and sets it next to Hattie. "Listen!" he says in a stern voice. "Don't you understand that all this happened to other people? Only incidentally to you!"

"Yes, of course," Hattie says miserably. "I know. But thinking of it that way is too much to bear. Thinking of those other people. It's better to be angry and curse the Germans. After all, the dead are dead now. But the killers can't die. They hang on. Their possibilities are always with us. Don't you see? They are saying to us, 'This, *this* is what people are capable of.' I curse them for showing it. Curse them for being it. How do they expect us to go on?"

"Who is they?" Stanwood asks strictly.

"They is the world. And us is you and me. The fathers and the mothers. The people who are supposed to carry on the loving and the giving. That's what it is, you know. A poison went into the atmosphere. Just as when an atomic bomb explodes. Each generation in turn will be sickened, poisoned with disgust for the human race."

"It wasn't the whole human race though, darling." Lillian begins an association of comforting thoughts. "Only the Germans."

"But they were—they *passed* for human beings. What does that *say* about human beings?"

They all talk at once. The assault of the room on the wall—"Stand still. Be firm, can't you!"

"There are so many other models," Lillian says.

"Yes. There are other models. And we're always watching for them. We're always watching the way other people live. Because we have no idea ourselves how we ought to

84

do it, we keep watching to see if someone else has had a hint. We're like unprepared children in an examination room. Driven to cheat, to spy out what the other person comes up with. Everything depends on the answers . . ."

"Who is cheating?" A small worried flush begins to mottle Lillian's cheeks. "That's an exaggeration again."

"I meant to exaggerate. For instance, if a woman is pregnant . . ."

They laugh. "Who could that be?"

"A mother is like a goddess to a child!" Hattie says. "What assurance can I give him? Where does the mother get her assurance from? What are we supposed to be passing *on?* What are we doing?"

Ezra has been narrowing his eyes at all of us. He's looking for us in his range finder.

"I do see that it happened to other people," Hattie says. "Once in a while I can bear to see it." She turns to me. "Do you remember what that woman said about the forced marches of women, and there were pregnant women on the marches? Do you know—" she appeals to the others again —"what it is to have to march in your eighth or ninth month? You have to hoist that weight between your legs, and if you keep it up your muscles start contracting—it's almost a kind of labor."

Hattie turns to me again. "And the ones who couldn't keep up were shot, she said, remember?"

I feel myself nodding stiffly. Even *The Thirty-nine Steps* again would have been better than this. . . .

"O listen! If a pregnant woman is shot, does the baby live, and slowly poison in the corpse? Or, if she's shot through the belly and the baby dies does the mother live, a living coffin for the dead child . . . ?"

85

"O Hattie!" Lillian cries.

". . . Then they got to the camp, and there was spotted fever there, and the pregnant women who survived gave birth on the cement floor there . . ."

"O Hattie . . ."

"Can you *see* how it happened to another woman? I can *feel* it in my body how it did. Every muscle in her is beating out the birth and yet she wants to hold back, to stop up the bowels of birth because she knows . . . what did that woman say, Jean?"

"The baby was bitten," I answer—I am drawn in—"the moment it was born, by the spotted-fever lice . . ."

"And the guard was watching, didn't she say?"

"By torchlight, she saw his booted feet . . ."

"He wanted to see how life began, he said. . . ."

Lillian covers her eyes with her hands. Stanwood holds his head. Only Ezra is still looking, eyes narrowed.

"Where are you every day at five when those witnesses speak?" Hattie demands of him. "You're out photographing telephone wires, aren't you? Arranging verticals and horizontals. About as far away as you can get. . . . And Lillian, when she's not typing in an office, is lugging your portfolio around for you to art editors, and Stan is selling TV sets, selling them . . ."

"Stay with the dead too long and you're dead, too," Ezra says deliberately. "Life belongs with life."

Slowly Hattie comes round. "Yes." She nods her head. "You're right. What's wrong with me?"

"O can't you make her stop watching, Jean?" Lillian bursts out. "It's so bad. So unhealthy. Those poor, poor people. It's horrible."

I light my cigarette. Did I start smoking again all of five minutes after your letter about Erna came? "I certainly agree there's no point in watching."

Lillian adds hastily, "But I'm so grateful that you watch with her, Jean. At least, if she insists on watching, she's with you."

"I suppose it's because I'm home," Hattie breaks in, in a dreamy voice. "Me with my morning sickness, and I have to be close to a toilet every fifteen minutes. And watching every day at five and hearing about those suspended lives. Cut off like that. I was wrong about them. They don't go away, either, like old people's deaths do. These hang in the air, too. I feel them continued in my own self. . . ."

Then suddenly and passionately she says, "I envy you, Jean! You're so lucky to have work you can do at home. You can be a woman and be where a woman should be, but still you can be different."

This makes no sense to me. What is the need of a woman at home if there are no children and no husband? But Hattie says this with so much wholeheartedness that I don't argue. I have my mask ready and I put it on, simple and stylized and very necessary. "No, Hattie, I envy you. You can allow yourself to sleep late and your world doesn't fall apart. I can't allow myself to sleep late. Without my disciplines I'd fall apart. Every morning I say to myself, 'What's it to be? Down the drain or up and work?' "

I am prepared for the stab of loneliness, which is the price always extracted at such masked, role-paying moments. What I am not prepared for is the wave of real envy that I feel. I envy Hattie her pregnancy, early-morning nausea, and everything. I want her child. It frightens me to hear this so clearly through my own speech to Hattie. "Down the drown or uk and wuk. I uk and wuk because I don't want to go down the drown . . ."

In the same dreamy voice as before Hattie goes on, ". . . Because I'm at home. At home, the housewife, with no escape except by bursting through the membranes . . ."

We yawn and fidget while she lists her other reasons. Because the child growing in her (who is he, she wonders, who?) has shaken loose her own taken-for-granted sense of knowing who *she* was. Some heretofore buried tendency to mimicry, some temptation to abandon herself, like an overloaded ship, sends her forth from the capsized body, heavily beached on the bed, to other lives.

"Do you remember Dr. Albert, Lilly? I remind myself of him . . ."

Lillian explains to me, "He was our dentist . . ."

"Already old," Hattie says, "when we started with him as kids. He had no new patients, just old ones and sometimes their children, like us. His equipment was old, his cabinets and all his little instrument filing drawers needed paint. His nurse was gone, his wife was dead. He was alone in his office all day, trying to pry out from his patients' lives something that would plug gaps in his own. 'How is your daughter's leg?' he would ask somebody. 'How is your brother doing away at school? I have a friend,' he would say, 'whose sister didn't marry for a long, long time. She waited and waited and finally . . .' It was more than passing the time of day. He needed long talks, long talks, and he took his time about pounding stuff in his mortar, or working the silver compound in his palm . . ."

"I remember he had creased, fleshy palms . . ." Lillian said.

"He was home all day, like a housewife. People saw him at *his* place, among his battered utensils, his little cooking flame. No wonder he tried to jump out of his skin into somebody else's. Didn't he horrify you, Lilly?"

Lilly weighs it for a judicious moment. "No-o-o, I suppose I thought he was a little slow . . ."

"When I give birth I'll move up a notch. Firing a shot, the gun recoils—back to the last generation," Hattie says. "I know this, yet I already love my child, my son, who will do this to me."

"To me also," Ezra says.

"To us," Hattie adds with a tender smile.

"Prepartum depression isn't recognized," Ezra says, bantering. "You don't get points for it, Hattie. Only *post*partum . . ."

"I'm carrying life—" Hattie goes on—"but I'm out of it myself, is what I mean. I'm suspended, like some kind of heavy balloon, over the living and the dead. I'm like Dr. Albert."

"O Hattie!"

"I sit at the window and I say, 'I'm like you, Dr. Albert.' I squeeze meanings from passers-by. I call through the window to the fairy in tight green chino pants, 'How do you live? Do you see relatives? Feel remorse? Wish for a son?' When the old lady up the street passes I say, 'What do you hear from your son, Lulie? Does he write . . . ?' "

A long letter, quoting conversations. I make use of the foursome when I come home. I can write you about them, last thing before the empty-bed blues. The foursome are safe. I need never refer to Erna at all. It can be Hattie's self-pity I write about, not mine.

". . . Ezra, who photographs only abstractions, never faces, must listen to Hattie's minute picturings of the witnesses' facial expressions. He squints his eyes while he listens, blurring the details out of his focus as fast as she can put them in. . . . Stanwood looks stolidly suffering. . . . Lillian worries, and strokes and fingers Hattie's hair and arms, does everything but listen for the fetal heartbeat while this goes on. . . .

"Forgive me, darling, if this sounds as if I am trying to make jokes about the horrors. There is something about the efforts of the foursome to make the horrors human-size so they can enclose them, grow around them. Something so damned irritating—and touching. I think one reason I can bear the second coming of the holocaust into my life is because the foursome surrounds it. . . .

"Lillian, anyhow, is a recuperator. She can't keep indignation or any mood long. She changes her style. Nature's lesson to her daughters. Don't argue. Beguile. Change your face and style and make-up and temperature. Dance with veils and without them. Be seasonal. . . .

"She is so glad I am watching with Hattie, but doesn't know to whom her thanks really belong. . . . Hattie pries at people's lives like her old dentist. . . . She has seen you, darling, look up at my window each time before you come up. . . . Why do you do that? Do you want to see if I've been X'd out of your life? How would you feel if I were?"

When I am finished, I take up my single-edge razor. What does not belong—the self-pitying touches, reproaches, other guilt-raising messages—gets slit out from the letter like bones from a fish. Then carefully I paste the top of each page of my letter to a white undersheet, lining up the undersheet and my letter overlay so that the cut-out spaces and the little drawings I begin now will register perfectly. With my finest crow-quill pen I begin to draw my naked lovers, one couple to a space, in the attitudes of love we like best.

Let Erna open this one "by mistake" if she dares. . . .

The moment I am finished with these little drawings I feel a great desire to tell you about Jesús.

I found this lost boy, I want to say, and I brought him home so that he can at least be lost in a safe place. I took him to my bed and let him come onto me and into me—because he's lost. But I'm not really finding him, as the joke goes, and I think he's making me lost, too.

Twelve |

My doctor is a woman. No special reason. When I first moved here I called New York Hospital to see if they had listings of doctors in my immediate neighborhood (maybe it was all the crashing demolition; I thought it would be nice to be able to call up someone if anything happened) and they gave me the number of Dr. Louellen McNiece. Her office is in one of the grand brownstones. Fireplaces and wood paneling and Turkish rugs on the floor. She shares it with two older women doctors whose patients have white hair and wear magenta satin hats. In the shared waiting room of Dr. McNiece and her associates, I am of the youngest generation.

From time to time I have some pain in the lower right quadrant—as Dr. McNiece refers to it—of my belly, and I go to see Dr. McNiece. She probes it, inside and out, measuring with her rather sharp-nailed finger tips the size of my right ovary. It does not always throw off the infertile egg cases, and it occasionally becomes encysted with them. It is nothing to be alarmed about, Dr. McNiece says;

most women complain of discomfort in the lower right quadrant, but it should be watched.

"What is the worst that could happen?" I ask.

"The worst is that it might develop a real cyst."

"And then?"

"And in that case, the ovary would have to be removed."

I sit cringing over my sobs. Because these are the offices of women doctors, filled with women patients, I feel I am breaking some taboo. Humiliation is almost stronger than my fear.

Dr. McNiece asks in brisk astonishment, "Whatever is making you cry?"

"It sounds to me like sterility."

"Nonsense! There are two ovaries."

"But if one is removed, then there's only half the chance of pregnancy, isn't there?"

"That is not necessarily true."

"How does it work again—is it every other month a different one functions?"

"No, it's not even always quite that way."

"But in any case, there's something about the possibility of having an ovary cut out—" I'm off again, stuffing a handkerchief abjectly into my mouth.

Dr. McNiece wears expensive, well-made clothes—heavy tweeds in winter, linen and silk in summer. She wears them with the peculiarly dowdy air of a woman who has more important things than clothes on her mind.

"Don't tell me you are like those primitive peoples who can't bear to have their hair cut or give up their nail parings?" Her blue eyes are perfectly clear and un-ironic. She believes she is joshing me out of some foolishness.

"Not nail parings—my ovary, Dr. McNiece."

93

"First of all, it may not have to be removed. You started this, remember, by asking what would be the worst that could happen. Even if it did happen, that still might not preclude your having children. Besides—there is such a thing as a population explosion—how many children do you feel you have to have?"

She writes out a prescription for a sedative. Her practiced hand pours out the illegible scrawl. She is a free lancer too, but in an extroverted profession. She is on the clinical staff of a large hospital; she is one of the staff doctors at *Time-Life-Fortune*; she has a busy office practice, and in her spare time she takes fascinating trips. This summer she is going to Egypt with two women archeologist friends.

She has no husband and no children, nor—her life declares—does she need any. Under her well-cut clothes, it is possible she carries no ovaries. Perhaps one or even both of her breasts have been cut away, or even the entire reproductive system may have been removed. It would hardly matter to her so long as the disease had been arrested.

She dismisses me with an amused, brisk glance that seems to say, "Haven't you heard—women have the vote!"

This time I have left a flask of urine with her. She is going to send it to a lab and have it injected into a rabbit's ear. My problems are not without their humorous side. Having asked her to reassure me that I can still become pregnant, I am also asking her to reassure me that that is not what I have become.

Not long after, I receive a message from Dr. McNiece—which does not get buried under Hattie's manuscript bulk—brief, and admirably to the point:

"Dear Miss Lamb: Negative. Very truly yours—"

Thirteen |

This morning three bulky pieces of mail. Galleys and jacket proof sheets from the typesetter's. A new manuscript from Dodder & Co., which I'll send back. I won't have time for it, even though my weekends now are free. And another two-pounder from Hattie. . . .

My desk is awash with manuscript. Which belongs where? I have the hysterical notion that I ought to design Hattie's letter and send it off to the copysetter, ink some erotic drawings around the margins of Chemical Affinities, Vol. II, sign it "love and kisses," and send it to you.

Once, when I had been telling you about the sheer tonnage of Hattie's mailbox revelations, you suggested lightly, "Why don't you counterdiary her?" Maybe I've done just that without knowing. Pages of my own diary, such as it is, things I'm sure I wrote down at some stage or other—are missing. At least I'm sure I meant to write them down. Maybe I sent them to Hattie after all. Or even to you, Loftus. Maybe they're stuck to a tissue layout somewhere on a copyholder's table at the Newark Offset Printing Plant. Or appended to an index, blurting out their lacks and needs amid the tight-packed, eight-point lists: Abercrombie, Abolitionist, Academy, Adams, Admiralty, Agassiz. . . .

On the other hand, I've received messages from Hattie —I think—that seem indistinguishable from my own. For instance, whose two-page confession of pica type, triple-spaced, is this?

. . . It's not as if I'd been a frightened child. I was a sturdy, sassy kid. The hellion of the family. The acter-outer, the talker-upper, the emotional throwback, the one who spoke with flying hands and raised voice in a family of soft-spoken, folded-hands folk. All the childish things, for example, that didn't frighten me. (I could list—stern uncle, bullies I physically fought, my skinny legs with more dark hair on them than I ever liked, and a best friend who was fair and hairless and looked more like my mother than I did.) And now, after escaping all that business, after walking through these small knives of childhood with good courage, now, when there should be no doubt of my grabbing life by the tail—because, I always thought, what's there to be afraid of—sickness? Old age? Death? Ha! Hey and ha! Those were the terms handed out to all the great ones. And they were good enough for me. I was finishing that, rising up from the child's bed of thorns and would become . . . O a singing bird, a garden with fountains. One year later, I was drowned in terror.

When I started to write this, I thought I would call myself Heart's Witness. To show how I was there. I thought I had the right because of my injury through terror. If I am not a Heart's Witness, then what am I, with my terror? If I found myself sending money and joining committees I would know what I am. A sympathizer. But I do nothing. I am paralyzed, in terror. I am an empathizer then, a mystical participator, the kind who claws her skin and screams "Stop them!" to the grinning men around a street fight.

Paolo and Francesca read about love, and loved. Do I really believe it's possible to hear about terror and be terrorized? Heart's Witness, I secretly call myself. I say this only to you. . . .

Is that Hattie's? Or is it mine, dating from a period when I was typing my diary, in order not to be seduced into hours of calligraphing my own morning wake-up ruse? Some of it fits me still. When I hear my name, "Miss Lamb," I feel a tugging of the rope. "Miss Lamb to the slaughter!" Not as victim, I never thought that, but as witness.

On another bit of paper:

Why do I have this feeling that I've imagined you? Because you are perfect for me. Too perfect. I'm like a child who invents a companion out of loneliness.

This is Hattie's:

Just one more thing. When Ezra and I decided to come to New York, because that was where he could work best, we took last looks all that spring. We watched the stream cracking behind the library. It smelled sweet. It was that time when all the trees seem to stand like naked men and women in a drizzle of birch catkins and green-oak flowers. We knew there were no birds in New York except sparrows and pigeons which pecked, we heard, at offal in the streets. We just stood and looked. We weren't sorry. I don't know why I had to tell you this. . . .

But whose is this?

I tell myself my time was out of joint. I philosophize about the time, the Zeitgeist. But does that account for everything? My dry life? My metronomic ticking away?

97

My life does not flow. I cannot make it flow. But is it the Zeitgeist? The truth! Whatever I did I did to oppose someone who expected something of me. Let me confess it. Anyone would have done. The passing years meant nothing while my opposition lived. Disapproving of everything I did but there, giving meaning. When my opposition died, that was the terror. Be honest. My life then had to justify itself. I became a ritualist. I asked for nothing but my ritual. My discipline. My work. My Loftus (ah, so it's me). *My weekends. But I want more now. I have been seeing more clearly. To be exact, I want to be Loftus' wife. Loftus is in despair. Hold off, he tells me. Don't, darling, put these pressures on me or I'll go mad. His wife is sick. Terrified at the thought of abandonment. She has never learned to be alone. I have. Therefore? Let us not be cruel, Loftus begs. His wife has known about us for years, perhaps from the first, is resigned to everything, makes no demands, accepts without complaint the weekend absences. . . .*

(But I don't understand this. Whatever made me think, at whatever point I wrote this, that Loftus and his wife still lived together?)

. . . asks only that nothing be disturbed. That is the ritual on which she depends. But I am adamant. I cannot bear the dryness of my life any longer. It's not enough, with these images of the dead of night around me again. My life needs to flow. Only if it flows can it pass over the horrors. And for that it takes another soul with me. More than one. Husband, children, relatives, in-laws, servants. Attics crammed and roof bulging. The whole Victorian stench and tangle. Whatever made any of us think we could make it alone?

*Every month is precious. Maybe all I have left is the
time of Hattie's term. How can any woman know? I have
given Loftus my word we will never see each other again
if he does not take steps.*

A letter from you. Loftus and Erna going over everything. Meeting again next weekend. During the week,
writing each other. Reviewing everything. Understanding
What Happened.

Erna, sitting at your desk, has mistakenly read some of
my letters, thinking they were memoranda from you to
her. No doubt one of these days a page of Erna's self-
examination will be mistakenly enclosed in your letter to
me. Only a question of time.

Fourteen |

"Jesús, listen! Don't think I'm saying this because I don't want you to come here. I do. But you've got to find someplace to stay. Someplace that's solid and regular. Not just a furnished room you'll hate to stay in. A small apartment, and we'll go to the Salvation Army and you can pick out your own furniture. I could help you pay for things, Jesús, till you find a job and can pay part of your own way. Or no, listen! Something much better than any job you could find now—school! You could study, and see what goes on in a world that's much bigger than Central Park and the subway and downtown. There are places that have classes for people who want to go on with their education . . . not kid stuff. You can find out what interests you, and work toward that. . . ."

He looks around. "You mean get an apartment like this?"

"O like this . . . listen a minute, Jesús. You have to have a very good job to pay the rent on an apartment like this one. Later you can. After you study and find what you like to do and get to be good at it."

"So where? I'm not goin' back into Spanish Harlem."
He collapses into a chair, deflated.

"Look. Take your shower. We'll work it out. We'll think about what you can do, and it will be a place that you like or we won't do it at all."

While Jesús is in the shower, I pick up the *Times* and run through the apartment-renting section. From Jesús' point of view, even from my own, the ads are impossible.

When Jesús comes out of the bathroom his mood has changed and he is full of interest again. "Did you fin' somethin' nice?"

"Not yet."

His expression folds up again.

"It's not going to happen in just a few minutes, Jesús. We'll have to work on it. Maybe, to start, the best idea would be a young men's residence."

"What's that? It don' soun' too good."

"Why not?"

"Somethin' like reform school?"

"Not at all like reform school. Just that there are other young men starting out, trying to make their way, and it's cheaper than a good apartment, but it's well kept up, and there'd be some other young men around for company."

"I'd rather be with my buddies."

"No, no buddies! On your own!"

I ought to have bitten my tongue before I said that. Jesús' face sets.

"Listen, Jesús—it's never good to try to work out problems late at night."

This astonishes him. "How come? I'm always workin' out my problems at night."

"How about some sleep, though? Then you'll be fresh

and have breakfast in the morning and you can think what you'd like to do. I want to help, Jesús."

He gets into bed and I say, like a cheerful nanny, "Now get a good night's sleep. I have some reading to do. See you in the morning!"

He turns over, takes two deep breaths and is asleep.

I look at the ads again, throw them down in disgust, wander around my apartment wondering if a place can be made here for Jesús (but thumps from Mario overhead warn me that a place cannot be made), pass my desk and without thinking, sit down again to Hattie's manuscript.

All the while I read, I ask myself why I bother to read. Some people can't bear to waste food or drink or an encounter that might lead to sex. I can't bring myself to waste this account of Hattie's life. Because it's there.

"How We Began as a Foursome." I read the title. God knows I'm not hungry for this, but I read:

The best way to explain how things started with us— my sister, Lillian, and me, and her husband, Stanwood, and my husband, Ezra—is to tell about the scare we all had in the car that night.

This is how it went. There was a pause after the thing happened. Stanwood kept on going right through the pause. He didn't wait to see if anything was going to happen after the something that unexpectedly, seeing it was Lillian, did happen. He didn't wait for news from the moon, or to see if her uncle from Red Bank was coming, or to hear if she, elopement valise in hand, had fallen off the roof.

He proposed right away, in the front seat of the car. He expected, seeing it was sweet Lillian and love under the moon, a baby. To expect that was for Stanwood, as he was then, to expect to fall in love.

He refused to wait, though Lillian, hating to impose on a nice young man she hardly knew, gave him permission. "We can see," she stuttered, "about the curse. In about two weeks."

But Stanwood hurried. "There'll be no curse. Only blessing from this. Sweet Lilly."

Lilly was embarrassed for fear Stanwood had mistaken female language for unfeminine feelings. But seeing he was determined to make good come of it, either way, she fell in love in turn. My sister, as she was then.

Ezra, my Ezra, on the other hand, was fully equipped in the back seat. His pouches swung, his flash and picture-making machinery hung weightlessly all over his body. Then he began to feel the weight he supported and he eased himself down to the seat alongside me. I think he said my name, "Hattie." I think it was right after that I said, "I love you."

I hadn't ever, in my twenty-two years of life in that split-natured town, met anyone like him—much less gone to car bed with. I thought Ezra was a fabulous lover. Equipped. In his pouches were, still wound, rolls of film on which was recorded the world's image. What I had felt at the moment of joining with Ezra, I remember, was suddenly so well-connected. It came through the accustomed isolation with such warm force that it was easily taken for love. Later that had to be sorted out, too.

When I said, knowing it was far too soon, "I love you," Ezra narrowed his eyes. The air felt cool on all the uncovered parts. A shaft of moonlight, I remember, came through the rear window and Ezra narrowed his eyes. He was a photographer. I knew that as soon as I knew his name was Ezra. He never went anywhere, not even on a blind date, without his equipment. He was seeing my face as something that might or might not suit the camera's square. He was squeezing out everything except the composition I made. Yet the narrow look seemed something else. And it seemed to be what I had been wanting. That I, who had been critical, was now being criticized. That, plus the exhilaration of the joining to a man who went out shooting the world and whose last name, I thought then, was something like Zeitgeist.

I'd never had use for women's wiles. But when, from the bottom of the car seat, I whispered, "I love you, Ezra," and was about to go on to discuss marriage, they came anyway, like indulgent sisters, to my nuptials. "Shut up now," they advised me.

That was when Ezra began to explain his great ambition in photography. It was to travel. To live in New York and other places. To be not—he was stroking my hair which I then wore straight and rather greasy, it being exam time, and still bearing on my own body the partial weight of his, plus the equipment's weight—to be not, could I understand this, see what it meant to someone like him, not yet be—tied down?

"I do see it," I remember I said. "My great ambition for years has been to go to New York and other places. I long to get away from this preposterous town of women."

"What's wrong with women?" Ezra had been surprised.

"Well, especially these women," I'd added, to make it simpler. "This college town's women. I've lived in the town below them and I've lived with them up on the hill. And I don't like living in a place where the girls' school is

the center of the top and the rest of the people droop away like streamers from a maypole."

"Streamers from a maypole." Ezra even repeated words with narrowed eyes, as if seeing the picture they made. By then I felt he was getting nervous, so I asked him why he wanted to go first to New York and he said to shoot buildings and I said, "It fascinates me that you're fascinated by buildings." He asked me why, narrowing his eyes and shifting his equipment, and I said, "I suppose because I'm in love with you."

That was when he suggested we get out of the car to take a walk. "There's something about a man who shoots pictures that attracts women," he said in a modest tone. "It's some kind of an erotic thing." I could only agree.

"I got used to it," he said. "I recognize my feelings now. A mixture of well-being and alarm. I like to hear it, that someone's in love with me. I suppose you know. But in spite of—" he tilted his head back toward the car—"we don't know each other well."

It was not my fault that at that moment I felt really humble, which was the wiliest thing to be. I said, "You don't know me well. I have many faults."

Ezra said, modest and fatherly, that he suspected as much. He did add, more of a gentleman than anybody's father ever was, that he'd been thinking the same of himself.

It was some time, Lillian told me later, before she'd noticed our absence from the back seat. She'd had no chance to turn around since earlier when, suddenly aware that she and Stanwood (for the first hour of their acquaintance she had taken his name to be Standgood) had been a long while cocooned together, she lifted her head to listen. All *was deathly quiet in the back seat. Her skirt was above her thighs, her blouse open to the summer night. Stanwood's hand was resting for the moment on her right buttock, very hot on her breeze-cooled skin. There, also, the situation had rested. He, philosopher, Spinoza reader, so he told her, would not grab enlightenment. But he sometimes prayed, he said, that it might come to him.*

Cautiously Lillian had lifted her head and looked into the back seat. Her sister, that is, myself as I was then, with arms and legs lifted, had embraced to oblivion a broad, curved back which still wore its diagonal leather straps. At the end of one strap, the pendant Leica jogged. In total darkness Lillian saw Ezra, fully equipped, hunting for his picture. And Hattie was his flash.

It entered my sister, Lillian's, mind, she told me later, "We'll both be married soon." Then, peacefully, she turned and submitted to her ethical lover that proof of wisdom he so studiously sought.

She, afterward, was scared she was pregnant. Instead it was me, but that one miscarried. And still, Lilly is not pregnant.

Fifteen |

Erna is coming to see me.

That is what I tell Sostana. For the first time I am afraid
of what the neighbors will think. I am afraid they will
think, because you aren't coming, that we have broken.
I'm afraid their thinking it will somehow make it fact. After
being smugly silent about my private life for so long, I
now tell even Hattie that you are busy arranging divorce
details with your wife's lawyer, and that your wife is coming to see me about the children, against the time when
they will be visiting us both.

Hattie is full of admiration. "What a civilized and loving
way to do things. I think you are all being marvelous."

But Sostana is thrown back onto another bitter memory.
"The classic visit!" she says with a harsh laugh. "I, too,
made such a visit. Men!" She spits the word into my room
and I want to cover my work with my hands. Don't listen,
children, or you'll be warped for life.

She is having an evening drink with me. Mario has a boy
from school visiting him upstairs. We hear great clump-
ing steps now and then when one of them gets up from

the TV to go to the bathroom or get something from the refrigerator.

"Why do you want children?" she asks. "You're mad!"

"I don't have to know why."

"Let me tell you a story. Then, if you like, become very angry at me." She flashes at me her sad, dazzling, European smile. Her hair is fluffed around her long, bony face. Irrelevant, like a hat on a horse.

"Something I watched here—in this neighborhood—was how they wrecked the El. They burned it, with acetylene torches. You saw it, too, eh? There were golden showers under all that blackness. Everywhere, people watched, do you remember? I was fascinated, too. I might even have enjoyed it myself, some other time. Those strong men on the girders, eh? The blackness of the beams, the shapes of the wreck.

"But every time I passed a certain corner, the same words came to my mind. As if there were a wound-up mechanism in some part of my brain. The mechanism would tap out, 'It's the burning time.' I had just come back from Reno, you see? Six weeks and a day. I hated my husband, my dear. Still, when I went to bed at night I had to curl up like a fetus, my knees to my chest, to try to squeeze out the burning sensation in the pit of my stomach. Something burned, something *yawned* there, as if flesh had been cut away.

"One day I saw him walking in the street. My former husband. Only from the back, but I knew him. Everything I hated about him had disappeared. All that was left was everything I had eliminated from my picture of him in Reno. All that was there, for the moment without the protective shadowing of everything I hated, was everything I had loved. . . ."

I am waiting for Sostana's point to emerge and pierce me somewhere.

"Isn't that funny?" Sostana says. "Because you must realize, my dear, that when I was in Reno I was happy. All that dryness and heat, those endless, flat roads. Like a surrealist landscape. Like a Magritte, you know? Nothing bleeds there. One feels a marvelous euphoria. One is released from loyalty. You have made up your mind to disown your marriage. You are no longer—what shall I say? —*grafted* to qualities of the other person that you never really liked. What freedom! It's *that* freedom which gives the euphoria. The women joke about their husbands' revolting habits. After the euphoria comes the knowledge that the relationship is broken. Relationship is meaning. There is no meaning any more to Peter and Sostana. It took Peter and Sostana five suffering years to know each other. They will not know each other any more. What to do with all that knowledge? I know how he lifts a spoon, squints against light, makes love. What to do? Drop it, as if it were an object. Let it smash. Back to the void with it. Where there was meaning, let there now be none. . . ."

I am finding it hard to catch my breath. I can hardly follow what Sostana is talking about.

"What an arrogant bastard my Peter was. I am using Reno talk now. That's how we talked, when we sat in the living room of my little boardinghouse. It was homeopathic, fire with fire, and little was felt in all the burning. Afterward the blisters began to pull and draw. Burns over two-thirds of the body. That is the most one can suffer and still live.

109

And inside the rough, brutal surgery, so that one can only sleep with knees drawn up to the chest . . ."

She breaks off. "That is not even the story I meant to tell you. *Dio!* What a talker I've become! Forgive me. . . ." She flashes me a brilliantly sad smile and abruptly changes the subject.

"When is the wife coming? The classic visit," Sostana says. "I, too, made such a visit."

"It's to work out the details," I say.

"Of course. To work out the details. . . ."

It was Sostana who had suggested in the first place that the wife would visit me. All I did was agree to that.

"Yes, the wife will come, because it is more civilized that way."

"To arrange some details, because there are children . . ."

"Of course, because there are children, and there are details. And between the details, because you sleep with the man she slept with and bore children to, she will try to get very close to you . . ."

"I don't think so. I don't think Erna is that type . . ."

" 'What do you see in my husband?' That is what she will say. 'You will forgive me if I ask that . . . ?' You will answer, quite sensibly and rightly . . ."

"I don't think we ought to be discussing this . . ."

"Brava! But then, in spite of yourself you will add . . ."

"He's good, decent, kind . . ."

"Brava again. Do you think he is that to his wife?"

"Relationships are different. I don't know. I don't want . . ."

Sostana's eyes glint at me. "Why do you insist on marriage? Your situation now is perfect. . . ." Her voice wheedles, cajoles. "Do you think a woman, after marriage, can ever be . . . Aside from children, what earthly reason . . . And surely you, now . . . ?"

"I really won't discuss . . . !"

"Why do you need him? I ask only out of curiosity."

"I absolutely refuse . . . !"

". . . This aging piece of flesh . . ."

"You yourself wasted . . ."

". . . This deceiver . . ."

"Waster!"

". . . This deceiver, this *trompe l'oeil*, this *man!*"

"Waster! Depreciator! Inducer of psychological impotence . . . !"

"My need . . ."

"Bad guardian of the treasure . . . !"

". . . is greater . . ."

"You don't deserve . . ."

". . . than yours!"

Silence. The voices that have filled my room—ours, or echoes of other voices—have stopped. Sostana had become Erna. I had become the thief of Sostana's marriage. In the midst of this silence, a gigantic crashing to the floor. Mario or his friend is pinned.

I refill my opponent's glass. Her smile glitters at me. We settle ourselves. The standard on the podium bears the neatly lettered sign: DEBATE TONIGHT. Resolved: That the woman who has had the husband as not-husband needs to have him as husband more than the woman who has had him as husband needs to have him as not-husband.

In the auditorium, the student body, largely under twenty, leans forward with pad and pencil. Points will be given for clarity, diction, and the resilience of bodies over thirty-five.

Sixteen |

Jess Dorland from Parapet Press calls me.

"Are you busy these days?"

"Yes and no."

"I'm not asking you to have a drink this time, you know. I've given up on that. I mean manuscripts."

"I know."

"*Would* you have a drink one of these days?"

"Certainly I would. Not this week or next though. I'm very tied up."

"Okay. Back to manuscripts."

"Yes."

"Will you take one on for us?"

"If it's not—in a rush. What is it?"

"Brace yourself. Are you feeling like a woman these days?"

"I continue to faint at the sight of blood."

"I mean can you stand it if I send over something called *All About Feminine Hygiene* by a Wisconsin doctor who's eighty and feels very fatherly toward his patients? I'm actually reading, 'After toileting themselves, women should always wipe themselves with soft paper in a front to back movement, never back to front, so that particles of . . .' "

"Grand."

"You like it, do you?"

"Is there a lot on pregnancy in it?"

"Why, are you?"

"No."

"There are at least four chapters on pregnancy. Fears of, fulfillments of, ways of avoiding, ways of inducing . . ."

"You can send it to me, Jess."

"And a jacket, too. We'll need a jacket sketch before we get layouts. Something soft and feminine, natch. Don't give us any budding branches, for Chrissake, but that sort of thing."

"No budding branches," I agree. I am thinking that I will do budding branches. I will commission Ezra to go and photograph some, and maybe superimpose a profile, lightly veloxed, of Hattie at a window.

"I know the ideal thing, if they'd let us do it," Jess begins dryly. He is addicted to low-comedy office jokes, and it's my turn to ask, as straight as possible, "What's that?"

"Wrap it up in a sanitary napkin."

"But you couldn't print on that, Jess."

"Gee, that's right. So what we'll do is put the whole thing on microfilm, roll it up and stuff it in a Tampax inserter. How's that for a direct mailing? They won't even have to read it, just shove it up . . ."

"Very good. You won't be needing a jacket, then."

"Okay, okay, do it your way. Incidentally—" Jess pauses with mock tact—"it's ridiculous even to mention this because I know how meticulous you are in your working methods . . ."

"Yes . . . ?"

"Somebody—probably in our dumb copy department —mixed up a few pages of a novel manuscript in that science schoolbook you did for us. Some improbable love scene in a car—right in the middle of a chapter on plant reproduction."

I shut my eyes. I'm feeling giddy.

"So I told them," Jess says, "they say the sexual roles of men and women are changing. So why not plants . . . ?"

Seventeen |

Extra! Read all about it. Hattie is in everybody's day and in every day's body. She sends me the melting news. She has passed through the membranes that enclose her own and other people's existence (her thinking is more and more uterine). She says she more than *perceives* other people's lives—she *experiences* them. With distortions, of course. While one or two senses poke through the mucous-y bag, the others don't quite make it, so there are gaps. For example, she is not exactly Stanwood. But there are times when she feels she experiences his day at Bargainland.

"Sitting at the window today, I was in the whole thing of Stanwood's first day at Bargainland. . . ."

In Stanwood's case, it is through smell that she makes her way into his day. The loft smell of the boards, the smells of vinyl and porcelain and enamel, and walnut Formica veneer which covers the TV consoles and stereos. And Stanwood's own smell—of cigarettes, coffee containers and the combined smells of spicy hot dog and oversweet orangeade in the stand where he takes his lunch.

Other days, other moods. She can be in Lillian's day. At least the part of it that concerns Ezra. Lillian carrying Ezra's pictures around. Sense of looking. Lillian's eager looking. And the others looking. "O these men who are trained to see!" I gather she also means Ezra. In Lillian's case she sends me the thing itself. A composite scene made up of what Lillian has reported, plus what Hattie has intuited, or wished, or God knows what.

Eighteen |

1 |

"Loftus, my darling—

"May I send you more installments from time to time of the 4-some's history? It's coming into my mailbox by the twenty-pound weight. I won't send you the originals (you won't believe the *detail* in them). Just a distillation here and there of something choice. Darling, I don't mean that stupid flippancy. Hattie is pouring out her heart's blood and I'm sponging it up as best I can. It's all stored somewhere in the reliquary. The thing is, I have trouble finding a tone for these letters. I want to leave you alone to work things out. I *demand* from myself toward you that kind of patience and tact. But I also want to write you. And without drowning you in *my* heart's blood. So I'll write you the 4-some, okay? I'm not mocking them, God knows. Part of me envies their cosiness—like that art editor Lillian showed Ezra's pictures to—the one who said two is hard enough and four must carry some kind of blessing. But I haven't written you about that yet, have I? Or have

I? I *must* order my desk, while I have this extra time. I'll be so much freer later, for you . . ."

2 |

"Loftus, my darling—
"Here is a bit of Americana for you. Lillian and Stanwood first met at a downtown luncheonette in Fairmont. Seated next to each other at the counter, having their hamburgers and cokes with chipped ice. After they had passed the salt and pepper shakers and the cone-shaped sugar container that poured, upside down, like ketchup from a bottle, and the plastic cream jug with its cream-clotted retractable metal tab (I'm improvising, darling, but not very much), then Stanwood swallowed the last of his hamburger, wiped his mouth politely on the paper tissue he'd pulled from the metal dispenser and asked, 'Are you up at the college?'
" 'O no,' said Lillian. 'My sister, Hattie, is there. She is the student. She has a scholarship.'
" 'And you?' Stanwood asked.
" 'I'm a typist at Forten's Insurance.'
" 'I'm a salesman at Warbeck's Furniture Store. But I'm also a student. On my own, I mean. Are you also a student?'
" 'O no,' Lillian said. 'It's my sister who . . .'
"(This is *nearly* verbatim, darling, at least so far as the gospel according to Hattie is concerned. Lillian repeated the conversation to Hattie, who promptly at the time committed it to her total recall, and then one and a half years later writes it down and sends it to me and I to you

with about ninety per cent, for reasons of space, excised.)

" 'I mean are you a student on your own, in that way,' Stanwood said. 'Reading and inquiring, I mean.'

" 'I know what you mean.' Lillian said it out plainly because she understood what he would have liked to hear.

"(Hattie's note: 'Lillian never misleads. Even when she says two opposing things in one sentence, she means them both.')

" 'But I'm not, not in that way either. Whatever I learn it's from my sister Hattie, who tells me things. I'm not intelligent.'

" 'Yes, I think you are,' said Stanwood.

" 'Well, yes, I guess I am. But not a student.'

"Almost at once they were a foursome. When Stanwood asked Lillian for a date she said, 'I will if you bring someone nice for my sister.'

" 'As nice as I am?'

" 'Yes, I meant to say that,' Lillian said. Not flirting, only regretful. 'But my sister,' she reminded him, 'is up at the college.'

" 'For a college girl, a college boy,' Stanwood said promptly. He called his friend Ezra, who came the twenty miles by bus, his ancient car having broken down, with his camera gear.

" 'Stanwood's very, very nice,' Hattie had said to Lillian after their first double date. 'I think *Ezra's* very nice,' Lillian said. Each sister thought her own man superb from the first and hastened, guiltily, to assure the other that she had not been altogether cheated.

"But in fact, as the dates progressed, the couples no longer saw each other as separate individuals. The four of them made a four-stranded figure whose strands wove an intricate pattern. A sailor's knot, double-tied, one knot giving strength to the other. A circle squared, a moving corral. Hattie especially loved the idea of moving inside a moving corral. They could all exaggerate and say as many wild things as they liked, allow their tendencies to get out of hand, push too far to an absurd conclusion. Inside the moving corral, which was secure but never static.

"The fourth side of the square, the softly furred flap that shut them warmly in, of course, was Lillian.

"Lillian thought what a blessing that her husband and her sister, her two dearests in the world, should get on so, and she get on with her sister, and her sister's husband get on with her. With herself tied into such a stalwart knot, foursquare, she did not care if they went to Tibet, so long as all went.

"Looking forward was not enough. They were already, in spirit, there, already reaping the rewards of the move to the crowded, heartless, anonymous city. 'In these times, you can't do better for your children than to take them to the center of life. Even if that life is hard, even if sometimes what they'll see will be ugly. What do they see here? A town of nice enough people who'd as soon let the world go burn. We might as well be in the Middle West. They feel so safe in the middle. Like raisins in a cake.' Ezra, his mouth nearly watering, told them, 'I read that Puerto Ricans are pouring in at the rate of a couple of hundred a month. . . .'

"Darling, this is not much good. I am going to have to send you bits of Hattie's things verbatim or not at all. . . .

"We are both of us—Hattie and I—getting overliterary, the more we write. I suppose it comes from some drive toward scene-making connectedness that we all hope will give support to even the most flickering appearance of lifelikeness. In the end, the connectedness flourishes unduly, like the overgrown root system beneath the weevil-eaten weed."

3 |

"Darling Loftus—

"There's a kind of creative force to your silence. It seems to quadruple communications from Hattie. Her manuscripts grow fuller and fuller—just like Hattie herself. They slide over my table and carpet. Some of them have gotten mixed up, I think, in the ones I'm designing.

"Contrast to the fullness of Hattie's news—my radio destroys itself. Topples off its shelf (vibrations from the demolitions outside?) and smashes to the floor. I must buy another. I'll go to Bargainland for it, and let Stanwood make the commission.

"This is just a hasty note. I'm keeping very busy. Swamped with work. Write soon again, won't you, darling? A little more fully, if you can? Good-by for now. I must run to buy a radio.

"I enclose Hattie's account of Lillian's day."

They kept her waiting an hour and ten minutes in the drafty green anteroom of Photography Year. *When it was her turn, she followed a pretty young girl with a large black oilskin portfolio tied with ribbons at the top and sides.*

"I hope you had good luck," Lillian said, struggling to

get her own slippery album tucked under her arm. Her best blue sleeveless dress was rumpled with all that sitting.

"A waste of time," the girl said, doing something with her mouth, so that she looked as if she was about to spit out a very small seed.

The receptionist answered a buzz on her board and said, "Go in, please. Down the hall and last one on the right."

Lillian walked down the hall and entered a tiny office. Photographs were tacked everywhere on the beaverboard walls, and were piled in warped columns on the desk.

The man behind the desk was, Lillian at first thought, distinguished looking. He had a long pale face, a small, brown mustache, half-lens glasses, over the tops of which he watched her come into the room.

"Sorry you've been kept waiting," he said softly. He opened the album; and after glancing at the first photo he asked, "Are these your own?"

"No." It was tempting to blurt it all out, but she remembered what they had all decided and said only, "I'm showing these for someone."

"Your husband," he said, smiling kindly because she seemed so shy and nervous.

"No, not . . ."

He held up his hand to show she needn't explain. In spite of that she finished, somewhat surprised at her own restraint, ". . . not exactly."

He looked at every picture in the open-ended, double-acetate pages of the album. He took his time, studying seriously while his finger tips were under the page, ready to turn, and not stopping until he came to the last picture in the book. Even then he did not shut the album, but went

123

back to look at something at the beginning. Lillian, for a moment, thought he might start the whole looking over again.

Finally, he looked up at Lillian. Even then he did not shut the book, but kept it open at the two facing photographs of a line of graduates proceeding along the top of a hill at dusk, carrying ropes of ivy on their shoulders. Ezra had tried to make them look like women of an ancient culture carrying out some mysterious ritual, and for this, of course, he'd blurred out their faces.

"Now," the editor said, "tell me something about the man who took these pictures."

Lillian thought he perhaps ought to have told her something about the pictures first, but she tried to comply.

"He's . . . well what do you mean, Mr. Rigren, tell about his personal life?"

"Not unless you want to." Mr. Rigren smiled and leaned back. Seeing Lillian's puzzled face, he added, "Well, let's say, not unless it has bearing on his work. Does it?"

Lillian wondered. And since she could not arrive at an answer for herself, she decided to tell Mr. Rigren all about them and let him decide.

"Ezra, the man who took these pictures, is my brother-in-law. He's married to my sister, Hattie. The four of us, Ezra and my husband and Hattie and I, come from a little town in Massachusetts—" she pointed to the picture —"where this college is located."

Mr. Rigren looked at the picture again, over the top of his glasses.

"And we . . . we decided to come to New York," Lillian went on, wondering how close she was coming to giving the information that was needed in order to sell

Ezra's pictures, "mainly because Ezra was very interested in photographing things in New York, the buildings and the New York scenes."

When Lillian heard herself say this much, she felt reassured that she had come very close to what must be wanted. She was talking about what had bearing on Ezra's work. Anyone in New York who would be interested in buying Ezra's work would be interested in knowing that he planned to do a great deal of photography about New York. And, in fact, Mr. Rigren was leaning back in his chair, which so filled the tiny office, and looking at her with deep concentration. Looking over the tops of his half-lenses, which gave the impression that should he shift his glance lower and look at her through the lenses, he would be seeing her in another way. So that it seemed to Lillian that he was listening with one single, deep concentration, but could at any moment also be watching her, it seemed, in two ways.

"Our apartments are just a few streets away from each other," Lillian said. For a moment she paused to wonder what bearing that had. She had said it, and since she usually trusted what she said, she was sure the bearing must be there someplace, and at last it came to her. "We are all watching his progress here, my husband and my sister and I. Every night, when the takes are dry, we look at them. We live just off First Avenue, close to where the Third Avenue El used to be," she explained, forgetting that any New Yorker would know what she, the newcomer, had had to memorize. "And Ezra is photographing the demolitions."

At those words, Lillian felt a great surge of pleasure. That, of course, was it. She had gotten, by one way and another, to the main, important thing. It was Ezra's work, and it had bearing on how they lived, and how they lived had bearing on Ezra's work. And that was, of course, the important thing that she knew all the time, every day. It was what gave them all such joy, and yet, funnily, she had almost been unable to think of it when someone asked her, "Tell me about it." She had to come around quite a long outside way to what she knew inside herself all along.

"Ezra is photographing the demolition of the old, pre-war New York," she said. " 'As above, so below,' he says. He says the chaos and disorder in the sky (meaning the demolitions) are like what goes on on the ground. He also says the El was a road, and when they took that away it created the need for some other kind of thorough-fare (he doesn't literally mean a highway or another road though, you know), of letting people freely move around. And then there's terrible disorder on the ground. Because of the land boom and speculation going on. The East Side was mostly a poor people's neighborhood, and now they are dispossessed. You can see the X's on the windows where people have had to move because they are raising the rents in our part of town and because 'Green side, gray side,' Stanwood says, my husband, meaning the dollar bill, 'all around the town.' And Ezra is trying to get all of that in the wreckings."

Lillian stopped and waited to hear if Mr. Rigren might want her to go over some parts of what she had said, might perhaps want to jot them down on his pad, which he had been slowly pulling closer to himself on the desk.

"That's fascinating," Mr. Rigren said, though he wrote nothing.

So Lillain knew he had gotten it all then, first time, and there was no need to repeat. She slumped a little in the *chair, as she had been sitting quite tall to recite the dignity of Ezra's doings. And she smiled broadly, with contentment. "Isn't it?"*

"Mrs. . . ." Mr. Rigren glanced at his appointment pad, could not seem to make out his scrambled jottings, and went on immediately, "did you like living in that little town with the big women's college?"

Lillian was surprised. But she guessed it had bearing and answered simply, "Yes."

"Don't you miss it a little? I mean, it must have been very green there—I don't mean the dollar bill—and, and simple and good in a way?"

"O yes," Lillian said.

"Mrs. Tarrant." He had suddenly remembered her name as he looked at her over his half-glasses. But at any moment, Lillian thought, he might switch and look at her another way through the bottom of his eyes. "Mrs. Tarrant, couldn't you and your husband go back there?"

Lillian thought now perhaps she should repeat some of the bearing, but instead she went on to another bearing.

"We are a foursome, Mr. Rigren. We are four-sided. And we make a container that contains us all. We came here to be that way and we wouldn't go back unless it was that way, too." She shook her head. "But we won't go back."

"Now, you said that he—" he tapped his fingers against Ezra's picture of the college girls on safari—"he came to New York to take pictures. All right. But why did you and your husband—?" He stopped, looked again at the girls silhouetted on the hill. "You mean you all came for that reason? The container?"

Lillian nodded slowly, and gave Mr. Rigren a little smile

of encouragement. She was quite willing to go over the whole thing again with him if he needed that.

"But what about your own lives? Yours and your husband's? You can't just settle for two sides of a container. You have to do what suits you, too, don't you?"

"It does suit us." Then she realized she had yet to speak of the biggest bearing of all. "Our town was pretty and clean, Mr. Rigren, and smelled lovely in the spring. But everyone was pretty much concerned with themselves there, unless they stopped just a little to gossip about what went on at the college. Somebody expelled for being with a boy in the amphitheater all night or something like that. Here the people in our building sign petitions. And there's all that's going on at the UN. And now the demolitions and the Puerto Ricans and all. It's all very meaningful to us. And it has," Lillian finished triumphantly, taking Mr. Rigren into her pleasure, as she nodded at Ezra's wide, dark picture, "bearing on the work, as you said."

Mr. Rigren at last closed the album.

"Mrs. Tarrant, we can't use your brother-in-law's pictures. I'm sorry. The fact is we use very few outside pictures. Mostly our work is done by our staff."

He looked questioningly at Lillian's face and added, "It's not that your brother-in-law isn't talented. Many photographers are. The pictures are quite good."

Lillian, from the shock, so opposite to what was expected, and from the long time waiting and from the heavy bearing of all the personal facts that had, even though she knew them so well, moved her in the telling, started to cry.

"Mrs. Tarrant, O Mrs. Tarrant, please don't. You shouldn't be carrying these around, you shouldn't be doing *this kind of thing. New York is no place for idealists. Why doesn't your brother-in-law . . . ?"*

Lillian, behind her handkerchief, said, "He does take them around sometimes, but he's busy."

"Yes, of course, at the demolitions. But your sister?"

"She's pregnant."

"O my." Mr. Rigren rose. "Mrs. Tarrant, I think you have every right to know, for it has bearing on the work, that I am unmarried, recently divorced in fact, and that my home life is lonely. I also would like you to know, in case you're crying from pride—there's always the chance that that is what lies behind women's tears, though perhaps not with you—that I don't dream of dishonoring you with pity. You have your foursome. That is a warm, enviable thing to have. It's hard enough to be two. To be four must, I'm sure, carry some sort of blessing."

Lillian had dried her eyes and was looking up at Mr. Rigren.

"Mrs. Tarrant, let me see you to the elevator. Let me carry these lovely pictures for you. Your brother-in-law is highly talented."

When they were out in the hall and Mr. Rigren had one hand courteously under Lillian's elbow, they were approached by a hurrying stout man, in white shirt and bow tie. He approached, looking elsewhere, and grabbed Mr. Rigren's arm when he was directly before them. And still, despite his urgent manner, he continued to look elsewhere most of the time—to the left, to the right, up at the ceiling, down at the floor.

"How about the dummy paste-up—I mean the dummy, Fred?"

129

"Every Wednesday I see free-lance artists, William," Mr. Rigren answered with slow hauteur.

"Well, all I can say is they'll be on your neck, Fred. I mean it's your neck."

While they waited together for the elevator, Lillian saw that Mr. Rigren's lips had begun to move soundlessly. It was as if he was suddenly hearing, as Lillian had done before, that what he knew as plainest and most basic fact, he had somehow omitted to say.

"The reason I do see people, *Mrs. Tarrant, is just on the off-chance that there might be some free-lance work that might somehow work in somewhere. It's my duty to . . . to see everyone who wants to come. I make a point of it. It is my job. Do you see that? Mrs. Tarrant?"*

What Lillian saw was that he was as lonely in his job as he was at home. She shook hands and stepped into the elevator. She did not in the least begrudge him her afternoon.

Nineteen |

Jesús is lying on my bed, half asleep, and I am lying beside him, his head on my breast, my hand stroking his hair, while I read:

Dear Jean—I don't know myself why I write you all this. Sometimes I think it's to impress on myself as well as on you that this and this exactly was my life. No other. It's so easy for me these days to slip out of my life into some- one else's. We say, glibly, "There but for the grace of God go I." What when there is no grace of God? I go. I keep going. I go there and there. Slipping—off to this one, to that one. Like in skiing. A sideslip. Without any motion or will of your own. You slip into another's position. There but for the grace of God and there is no grace of God, we see that there is none—so I go sideslipping into the life of that woman who gave birth in the typhus-in- fested straw. Sometimes I feel I am her more than I am myself. I feel myself moving toward her image the way the weaker field of vision in a stereopticon gets drawn to the stronger.

Listen, Jean, do you remember Miss Dorothy Elmtree? Was she there at the college when you were there? Do you remember her? I was her student helper for a year. And Mr. MacAdoo? I was kind of his protégée. . . .

Suddenly, Hattie's manuscript in my left hand, Jesús' springy hair under my right, seem to belong together. It's clear to me now. It's not to you, Loftus, that I should be sending these bits of Americana.

"Listen, Jesús, don't fall asleep just yet. Let me read you something a friend of mine wrote about her own life. You might find it interesting."

"Is your frien' a writer?"

"In a way. Listen . . ." I get up and rummage through the pile, trying to pick a good beginning. Never mind. Any beginning can do.

"Listen! This is about where she lived in a small American town before she came to New York."

"Don' read me about no hicks," Jesús warns me. "I am a city guy." Jesús points his thumb at his chest. "In Puerto Rico we lived in San Juan, too."

"No, not hicks, Jesús. This woman went to a college that was in her hometown. But this is how she thought about things . . ."

"I think I would be more interested to hear about some guy's life," Jesús says doubtfully, propping himself on one elbow.

"All right. That comes later. Now this is called, 'Her Background.' "

Hattie has, along the way into her manuscript, taken leave of herself as Hattie the first person, and has become

132

Hattie the third. I clear my throat and read without changes:

Hattie and her family lived in a two-story house. The back of the bottom story, with a wooden porch on stilts, edged a small river, more a creek, that in the old days powered the paper mills. The town's two industries were paper and education.

When Hattie thought about it, it seemed to her that her family, more than the others, was outside of the mainstream of the town. And this made Hattie proud. Because of the difficulty of it, and the independence. The fathers of the girls she knew worked either in the paper factory or at the college. If the latter, they might be maintenance men. Some worked on the grounds, sawing limbs off the big trees after storms, chaining them up, cementing and cutting the trunks. Some looked after the special equipment, the boats and archery, the tennis courts and hockey fields. A few did nothing but cut grass in spring term, rake leaves in fall term and, in the winter months that in New England straddled three seasons, cut and carried fireplace logs to the dormitory housemothers, each of whom had an apartment with a fireplace, a table before it for tea, and flowered drapery hung on a pulley. A few men were night watchmen, challenging young men still around after hours.

Hattie's father was none of these. He was a sign painter, and over the doorway of their house was a sign, painted by him, that said: E. MEWS. SIGNS PAINTED. *He painted store signs (the college requested the merchants to avoid neon), an occasional* TOURISTS ACCOMMODATED *to be planted on two shaky wood stalks by a trumpet vine on somebody's sloped front lawn.*

Hattie was a day student at the college. Which meant she lived at home and went to classes every day on her bicycle, spent the afternoon in the castlelike gray stone library, and bicycled home in the evening for supper.

One year she had lived in a dormitory. The dean had offered her the scholarship and encouraged her to accept it. "I wish I could persuade more of you girls who live in the community [it was always community, never town] to come and live with us. The exchange is of benefit all round. But most of all, and this is between us, Hattie, it does a world of good to our student body to know and live with girls like you. You are a wholesome influence. They may never have such an opportunity again." Behind this tactful statement the meaning was: "Let the rich observe you. Wear your home-sewn clothes and invite them to your clapboard house with its slip-covered rocking chairs. . . ."

Hattie did it for one year, did not like it and refused a second chance, although Dean Whitmore offered to increase the scholarship to cover the cost of textbooks as well as tuition. But Hattie did not like living with the rich girls. It was not just the cashmere sweaters being washed in cold-water soap in the bathrooms and then hanging, like steam-rollered effigies, on forms to dry. It was not the fur jacket or belted camel's-hair coat hanging in every closet, ready for the weekend. Not the expensive, idiotic night-gear—the red flannel nightgowns with lace jabots, the monogrammed pajamas, the Hong Kong silk robes and the loud plaid woolly ones. Not any clothes. If you lived in a poor town that harbored a rich girls' college, you

*knew all about rich-girl clothes, and senior-year convert-
ibles, and matched, colored leather luggage, and gold
bobby pins.*

None of that was anything.

*The thing was that most rich girls were not very nice.
Except when they were being nice which, of course, made
everything worse.*

*For instance, there were three scholarship girls in the
dormitory the year Hattie was there. Scholarships were
kept secret but, of course, everybody made them out very
fast, and the scholarship girls themselves were faster than
anybody. So the rich girls, having made them out, started
being nice.*

*"Look, I have these two identical sweaters. I distinctly
hinted to my aunt to send me a navy sweater for my birthday, but she thinks all college girls adore red. They're identical, really, so please, please take one, the shade's just marvelous with your coloring. The only reason, on second
thought, I guess I'd better keep this new one is my aunt
may decide to come up, which she has threatened to do, and
then like a good girl I'll have to trot it out."*

*When they weren't being nice they were being what
they called awful. They made a joke of it for weeks
when the floor maid, who was the mother of Hattie's friend
Frances, painfully lettered a sign on cardboard and Scotch-
taped it to the inside of the bathroom door: "It is not nice
for your clothes to leave them in the bathroom to dry.
They will get smells."*

*It amused them all term; it became the house joke.
Whenever there was a house guest to dinner who made
things dull, one of the girls was sure to lean toward her
neighbor, delicately sniffing. It livened up the meal. It was*

stored up to become a cherished college memory along with the idiosyncrasies of teachers and all who had faithfully served for little pay, to be dragged out again at reunions. "Do you remember Ada, the maid? The sign she put up? They will get smells! O tee-hee. And O ha-ha!"

So much for Ada's concern over the pretty things of the rich girls.

Hattie, of course, had laughed with the rich girls. How else could she have survived the year? But she knew she was not earning her scholarship. Dean Whitmore would have wished her not to laugh. To frown wholesomely instead. To say, "It is not right, you know, to mock the honest. Sophistication is the dressing dry hearts need." Or, in the language of the "community," which Dean Whitmore would have liked even better: "Ada's a real good-natured person. She wants for you to take care of your things because that's how she does for her own."

But Hattie had learned a thing or two in her scholarship year that would have disillusioned even Dean Whitmore. One of the things was that it was better to let the rich girls have their cruelty in jokes. Another thing was that it was better to allow the rich their sense of superiority. Spurious superiority was a safeguard. Meanwhile, honesty and humbleness could travel their ways in peace.

Over Hattie's protests, her mother had pressed on her a sum of money with which to buy new clothes for her year at the dormitory. So Hattie had bought soft sweaters and a good tweed skirt and hand-sewn moccasins at the campus shop, and had the bitter pleasure of an inquiry from one of the best dressed juniors as to where she had found that lovely pink pullover.

Her mother, that well-balanced woman, without envy

and without rancor, took pleasure in her daughter's pretty new clothes. And in her ancient black coat with the black potted brisket hat, she went to church and prayed to the Virgin to clothe them all in goodness and love. She was as innocent and good as Frances' mother, Ada the maid, was innocent and good. She believed that if one went among well-dressed people it was polite to make the effort to buy one nice pretty thing so as to look well among the well-dressed. The rebellious gesture, to wear sneakers when the rest wore their nylons and their calf pumps never occurred to her. Of extremes she could not conceive.

Two generations of cold Canadian slumber plus two of New England gentility had driven the Frenchwoman out. But Hattie had caught her again. She resembled the ancestors. She loved to throw her arms around. She minored in French and loved to say, putting her shoulder up to her dark hair, "O ça!" She looked at her placid mother in the wrap-around housecoat, searching for suppressed laughter around her mother's lips, for the eyebrow lifted at this precocious child. Echoes of Colette and Colette's mother Sido.

"O ça," she said. "Je m'en fou de tout ça!"

Her mother, at last, was reminded of an Aunt Hedwige her own mother had told her of.

Jesús interrupts. "What was those words back in the end?"

"That's French. *Je m'en fou de tout ça.* It means fuck all that."

"Well, you tol' me I was gonna *learn* sunthin' about American life!" he says indignantly.

"Right. No more French."

137

"Well, what did you read me that for, anyways?"

"I don't know exactly. What did you think of it?"

"I don' know."

"Do you want to hear more?"

"I'm sleepin' now."

Twenty |

The next night Jesús comes I ask,

"Would you like to hear more about that young woman and about her sister and their two boy friends?"

Jesús shrugs. "Not if it's gonna be long!"

"It's not long. It's about coming to New York. About people coming from some other place and making a home for themselves in New York."

It's become important to me—why is that?—that Jesús should consent to listen. I cajole. I rattle the pages enticingly.

"From Puerto Rico?" he asks dubiously.

"No. But from a little town. And it's confusing and hard for them."

Jesús sighs and props both our pillows under his head. "Okay. If it's not gonna be too long."

" 'Their Good-by to the Town,' this one is called, Jesús."

"You better hurry up," he says, yawning. "Before I'm sleepin' again."

I hurry.

✦ ✦ ✦

On one of their last weekends in Fairmont, the foursome went to the main part of town to have hamburgers and then take in the town's one movie, noncontinuous, beginning at 7:05.

They passed the idlers gathered at the jewelry store window, yellow-papered against the spring sun. At the end of the row of stores was the town's traffic circle, one lane leading out into the highway that spun through the valley, the other one climbing a slow grade back to the big old mansions of the town's first rich people. Beyond the mansions was a small pine woods and then the clear green of the first campus grass that went back a hundred yards on each side of a gravel road, unfurling from a tall, curly iron gate. The first building was set square to the road. It was the administration building, with a turret. Hattie's and Lillian's father had jokingly told them there were secret spiral steps inside leading to the turret roof for all the pregnant students to throw themselves off of.

"Is that true?" Jesús asks.
"Everything she writes is true."
"How about that."
"Here's more."

Hattie went back to the dormitory, where she had lived for a year, to say good-by. Deacon Hargate Dormitory, named for the Elder who helped build it on a succession of Mondays through the college's first year. His tithe of work to God, he said—holy work to build a woman's college.

The big, ugly, high frame house with porches, porticos, dormers, and gables was painted, to match its soul, dark gray. *There was no one home except Lisette who was, as usual, in her room, writing a letter to her boy friend. Lisette had been in love with this particular boy since her second year of high school and her father had sent her here to forget. But all she had forgotten, in the heavy atmosphere of letters to and from the Navy, was to attend classes.*

"O God, are you lucky to be leaving," she said to Hattie.

She was waiting to flunk out of all her courses, to be abandoned as hopeless by her father and to be free.

Hattie wandered down to the smoking room and picked up the copy of The Selfless Years, 1840-1847 *that always lay on the table there. The founding years. There were sixteen girls enrolled in the college's first year. The girls had worked like demons. They had hauled wood, helped to whitewash walls, scrubbed the classroom floors, boiled the communal college linen in huge vats on the lawn in front of Deacon Hargate Dormitory. The classes had been irregular. There were a few traveling teachers who stopped at the college and lectured on whatever came to mind— astronomy, Euclid, Greek art. The girls were in ecstasy. They froze in winter in their rooms and chopped their water from a pond. In summer they sweltered under the dormers, and harvested apples in the college orchard, and then, in the evenings, after lectures and readings, preserved them in the great basement kitchen. Their letters home were grateful. "Everyone here is so good to us. . . . We are taught as the men are taught. Not so regularly, it is true, Papa, but by the same standards and with the same respect for truth. . . ."*

Hattie loved their pictures. Those dark, indistinct photographs. In silly bloomers on the athletic field, grouped around the tennis net and holding on purposefully, as if they had just finished weaving it. In a bare and makeshift laboratory, huddled over a single microscope.

Though their letters were full of cheer and the joy of hard work, they remembered, when they faced the camera, something sad. What? That they were daughters. That funds from home might any time be diverted to a son or a new cow. That they were privileged, and much of the world in darkness. Many of them never married. Their education set them up for more education, and they became teachers—some, missionaries.

Hattie had picked a few of the girls—their serious faces swamped by rolls of black hair—as special friends. A Miss Eliza Fritch, who went to China and died of cholera at the age of twenty-seven. She mourned her. And a Miss Felicity (the intense, dark face was nothing like the name) Groves, who taught a while in India, then was drowned in a flood. The two young ladies, almost like sisters, had paired their thin, darkly clothed arms. One grasped a microscope by the middle of its neck, holding it out from her body a little way. The other lifted on her palm a model of the moon. They stared gravely at the camera, stiff-breasted, arms linked at the waist.

There was a third one as well. Whether she had befriended the other two, Hattie didn't know. She was on another page. A broad, placid face, a heavy roll of light hair on both sides of her forehead, like bright, rolled curtains. If it had been the custom of the time to smile at the camera, she might have smiled. She carried nothing in her hands, linked arms with no one, and stood at the center of a group of young ladies, sleeves uprolled in the scul-

*lery. Her broad face shone pleasantly with sweat. Her
name was not given. Her fate was unnoted. Evidently, she
had not become a missionary, or died young, or lived to
be an outstanding spinster. She may have married and
taught. Felicity and Eliza would have been friends. But it
was this bright-faced girl on whose shoulder Hattie, at this
moment, in the confusion of her feelings, could have rested
her head. She resembled, in fact, Hattie's sister, Lillian.*

"What do you think of that part, Jesús?"

"I thought you said this was somebody's life now."

"It is."

"Yeah, but it's all about like a hundred years ago. That's
too way back for me, you know? Otherwise I like it pretty
good I guess, I don' know. I'd like it better with more guys."

"Here's something with a guy in it."

*In Hattie's American Lit class Mr. MacAdoo, the tall
Hemingway specialist, was telling them about Scott Fitzgerald. He was embarrassed when he mentioned that the
writer had journeyed from the Middle West to the East.
And a little more uneasy and buried in the book when he
came to the theme.*

*"The theme, young ladies, was . . . the longing of the
. . . poor American . . . to join the ranks of the rich
American. And not, of course, only rich American but
Eastern too, and that, of course, as the term East has been
used throughout American literature to stand for refine-
ment and culture and with that a certain irony when one
examines finally what, actually, is the fabric of that so-
ciety, composed as it may, though not always, be, of at*

*best a thinness or sybaritism, or at worst of a kind of Phi-
listinism whose natural concomitant is cruelty and destruction."*

*Mr. MacAdoo coughed and shifted his shiny pants to an-
other corner of his desk. "I sound to myself somewhat
Jamesian this morning." And he laughed into his textbook.*

*"In short, we question the values of Fitzgerald, who
thought he was questioning the value of things even while
desiring them. . . ."*

*He stopped and looked around as if hoping his language
would take on a meaning in the ears of his listeners that he
found lacking on his tongue. "Princeton, of course, was the
symbol to him in his own youth. And later in the lives of
his characters."*

*M. J. Barnes raised a hand. "Was he self-educated, like
Hemingway?"*

*Mr. MacAdoo coughed. "He attended Princeton," he
said gently.*

*"O, Princeton." M. J. nodded with relief, as if a stranger
coming toward her on a dark night had suddenly turned
into a friend.*

*And when they were assigned to read "The Snows of
Kilimanjaro," Mr. MacAdoo's embarrassment was acute
as he asked the class, "What is the central theme of this
story?"*

*Mary Lou Ames, whose father was a stockbroker, said,
"It's about a man who has lost his will to live."*

"Very true," said Mr. MacAdoo. "Why?"

"That's what I didn't understand," Mary Lou said.

"Anybody? Why?"

And so Hattie gave them all the benefit of her week-

end's pondering and said, "He has lost his will to live as well as his creative drive because he has married a rich woman and he has been smothered and pampered until he has lost contact with real life."

There was a silence, interrupted by Barbara Bean's incredulous "Wha-a-at?" Barbara's mother's family owned steel mills.

Hattie knew that Mr. MacAdoo agreed with her, though he did not say so directly. Instead, as she was speaking, he gazed around the room to see how the students were reacting. They were two of a kind, his wandering gaze seemed to say, two furless animals who complained of the cold to the amazement of the pelted ones who found the climate very comfortable indeed. And therefore he knew Hattie's thoughts as well as his own and had no need to listen, or to comment. In fact, it was from one of the warm, insulated ones he had sought an answer. Hattie knew this and had waited also for one of them to speak. But no one had.

"The woman in this story," Mr. MacAdoo said, his face, now that he was finished with his looking, as bland as could be, "is one of the loveliest of all the Hemingway portrayals, I think. I submit that this presents a fine irony. The male, while judging the values of the female, at the same time knows that she is lovely in herself. There is the suggestion of her innocence in all this. She loves this man. Cannot see why she is not good for him. Cannot see why their life together is not good. Her love for him is good. Sex has been good. She is lovely. Long, lovely legs—" his face in the textbook once more—"and so on. She is, we know, a beautiful woman. And lovely and seductive and opulent and so on."

It was after that class that Hattie told Mr. MacAdoo that she was going to be married and would move to New York.

Mr. MacAdoo looked for a moment as if he wished he could teach her something, even more than the rest of the girls. "It's not that I don't agree with your reading of the Hemingway story, Hattie. I simply wanted to add the point that she is a fascinating woman. A true female. Seductive. Tempting. Her smoothness and silkiness and richness. Tempting!" Mr. MacAdoo's tie had swung off to one side, revealing a button gone from his shirt.

As Hattie waited, Mr. MacAdoo went on, "I'm sure you must know the story, Hattie, apocryphal but useful, about Fitzgerald and Hemingway? 'The very rich are different from you and me,' Fitzgerald said to Hemingway. And Hemingway said to Fitzgerald, 'Yes, they have more money.' Do you know that? Yes, I was sure you'd know that."

Mr. MacAdoo laughed softly and looked nostalgic, as if he missed his research days. "It may all be a matter of temperament, Hattie. Some people take rich folks harder than others. There's also the richness of the rich, Hattie. The richness, as in Jane Austen. . . ."

Mr. MacAdoo said, with a laugh, "I had a high school history teacher, a Miss Frodel, who took a marvelously know-nothing line with her students. 'Of course I enjoy pretty clothes and my car and lovely vacations,' she told us. 'All I ask is that everyone else be given a chance to enjoy the same things.' But it's not . . . you know . . . somehow . . . the same. . . ."

Mr. MacAdoo seemed just now to recall what Hattie had told him.

146

"*New York can be an explosive experience, Hattie. It can pry all your various selves apart. But marriage will be a kind of cement for you, too. Congratulations, that's really fine news. Give yourself to the experience, Hattie. Melt a little in the melting pot. And read Thomas Wolfe while you're there.*"

Hattie had considered for a moment confiding to Mr. MacAdoo that she might be pregnant. Then she decided not. All the same, she had an almost telepathic notion that, in answer to her unspoken confidence, he was suggesting, "Read Frieda Lawrence. She left four children and a husband so she could live. . . ."

"What do you think of this Mr. MacAdoo, Jesús?"

Jesús shuts his eyes and reflects on the scene that has just unfolded. Slowly he nods his head.

"Yeah, tha's pretty good. I could see he was after the buck myself. She's not so dumb."

"Don't go to sleep."

"Why not?"

"There's a little bit more."

"O boy."

Miss Dorothy Elmtree sat very tall and slender in her wheelchair. She lived in the only house on campus without front steps. A small house, whose front door opened onto a paved path between two square front gardens enclosed by white picket fences.

Miss Elmtree taught "Description" and "Advanced Description." In her tiny living room was a long, darkly polished oval table around which the girls in her classes sat. In the center of the table there was always a reminder.

That was what Miss Elmtree called it. In the spring, the re-
minder was a fresh daffodil or blue gentian. That reminded
of the romantic poets. In the fall, some red leaves. In win-
ter there were stones. And they, said Miss Elmtree, were
the bones of the earth and made one think of dry and diffi-
cult things. Of rolling with the stones, of going some-
where, of traveling even by wheelchair, of beginning a
hard and wearisome way from utter rock bottom, of Lucy,
"rolled round in earth's diurnal course with rocks and
trees and stones."

In the end, summer, winter, or fall, it was the roman-
tic view that Miss Elmtree was reminded of most.

She asked her classes to describe a concert or a painting
or a tree. And if her students described what was in
the piece or the painting, what the movements of the music
were and what happened to the theme, Miss Elmtree was
disappointed. What she wanted to read was that the music
reminded one of giants, or the painting made one lonely,
or that the tree was fleeing, all disheveled with leaves, the
death of winter.

There were always a few students who stolidly de-
scribed in program notes. "In the first movement the theme
begins softly in the violins and is taken up as a canon by the
flute. . . ."

"O is that all?" Miss Elmtree would coax up from her
wheelchair. "O young ladies, when I see that painting,
when I see that painting, when I hear that music . . ."
Miss Elmtree put her long bony hand to her cheek and let
her eyelids flutter.

Three afternoons a week, Hattie took Miss Elmtree,
who called herself "Ulysses the wanderer," for a walk. She

could walk, leaning heavily, shuffling her long feet on the path.

"What do I see, Hattie, a toadstool there?"

Hattie carefully propped Miss Elmtree against a tree trunk and stooped and broke it off for her, the thick spongy stem offering less resistance than a blade of grass.

"I see Alice every time," Miss Elmtree said. "Don't you?"

Then, without pausing she said, "I have heard from Dean Whitmore that you are going to be married. There!" she said, "that's bloodroot. I knew I'd seen it around here last spring. No, don't pick it for me, Hattie. It's not like mandrake, you know, which one ought to pull."

Miss Elmtree looked at Hattie with her eyebrows still arched in surprise, from when she had seen the bloodroot. "I am thinking of one of your papers, Hattie. The one on the Mahler symphony. You said it made you think of millions of suffering people. Do you know, Hattie, that I am one of the suffering ones? Well, yes, of course, what else would you call it? I've been crippled almost since birth. And yet I find, especially in the spring, so much that delights me. Isn't that odd, Hattie, did you ever think that one of the suffering ones might find life more delightful than the person who worries about the suffering ones? And you're going to be married, too. And where's your delight?"

"I am delighted," Hattie said. Though she knew that what she felt about Ezra was not delight. The pounding excitement in the back seat of the car, the excitement when he squinted his eyes at something that was like aiming a gun, popping a flashbulb, the explosion after all the tension of focusing and seeing and aiming.

And Ezra, for all his appetite for the pictures around him, was not delighted either. He worked too hard and too fast, running sideways, moving backward with his hands up to his face like an athlete moving to catch a football.

No, Hattie thought. She might not have any delight, but it was not anything she missed. And Miss Elmtree, who had all the delight in the world in four lines of poetry a student might tuck into the trumpet of a daffodil and bring to class, had not an ounce of the pounding excitement that was driving their foursome to New York.

"I've often thought," Miss Elmtree said, looking for more bloodroot, "I'd like to call my course, 'Delight, 101.' What do you think, Hattie?"

"You'd be forcing everybody to see things one way."

"Yes, that's right. I would. Or I'd be forcing them to choose only those subjects in which they took delight. Would there be a few students, do you think, Hattie, who could find nothing to write about then?" She looked up mischievously from the bloodroot, one long, pale hand against the black locust bark.

Hattie had to laugh. "I suppose I could find something."

" 'Delight, 101,' " Miss Elmtree said, as Hattie slowly pushed her toward the little white house. "O I should like that name in our catalogue!" She laughed, and her face became all puckers and her long nose whitened and lengthened and her yellow teeth shone. "And the advanced course will be 'Ecstasy': Prerequisite, 'Delight, 101'!"

She wore a fluffy bow under her suit, which she could pull to one side or the other, coquettishly under the left or the right ear. She pulled it now to the right, leaned her long chin on it, and looked at Hattie over her right shoulder.

"The metabolism, I am sure, Hattie, soaks up juice from delight, as rice does from bouillon. O I should have loved to be a scientist! I should love to be able to think about what reading the Lucy poems does to the metabolism. How does reading Shelley strengthen the retina?" She laughed. *"Moo, moo, moo. O but what a clumsy thing to have to wheel through a laboratory in this old chair, breaking bottles and tubes and crashing into tables where the little experiments are cooking up! Moo, moo, moo."* She laughed. *"Poor me, clumsy thing. Poor old Ulysses, mind-wanderer only."*

All the rest of the day, while Hattie made Miss Elmtree tea and started her fire and brought her into her small sitting room to read until the woman came in the evening to prepare her dinner, Miss Elmtree went on in the same way. "Moo, moo, moo, I should have been a pilot, too, Hattie, to seed the clouds for rain. What would the effect on the clouds be of two folios of Shakespeare? Say, Lear? Those would be tears that fell that day, not rain. I shall be an aviatrix scientess! Moo, moo, moo." Miss Elmtree laughed, jotting down notes for a catalogue description of "Delight, 101."

When I've finished reading, Jesús blinks sleepily and yawns. "I don' get it. That is sunthin' that don' make no sense to me."

"All right. That's enough for tonight then."

Loftus, I dreamt that Jesús stole from me. Took money from my purse. I tempted him. All the same he took it. His buddies lounged outside across the street, smoking under the street lamp, while he came up and asked if he could take a shower. I kept busy in the bedroom. When he was finished, I called through the bedroom door, "Let yourself out, will you, Jesús? I'm finishing up in here." The door slammed. I went out quite deliberately to check my big handbag that I had left lying on the table in the entryway. The large bills in my wallet were gone. I felt relieved! There would be no more fantasies of Jesús my son. He had stolen from me. The next moment do you know what I was thinking? How *like* a son. How like a *lover*.

Twenty-one |

I go to Bargainland, and have a chance to corroborate Hattie's vision of Stanwood's day. It is oddly exact.

Top floor. Bare boards, gloomy light, a warehouse look. Major appliances front section, then on back to consoles. Stanwood at the rear with a customer. Gray cotton jacket with big outer pockets, sales pad and green ballpoint pen protruding. His body looks stouter, his face puffier than I had noticed. I have never before thought of him as a salesman.

It is not a busy morning. Not pre-Christmas, not slow-summer-everything-must-go bargain time, not spring-stimulation-sale time, not autumn back-to-home-improvement time. A dark, rainy day. An ordinary, nothing-at-list-price discount day. The tone of the store announces it. Repeatedly, a dull, single-clappered "Bong!"

A salesman raises his eyebrows at me. I nod in Stanwood's direction. "I'm waiting for that gentleman to help me."

I browse among the brown square bodies that stand on tables or on their own squat legs. An army of silent orators. A few of us—dark-clad buyers—move among them. We look strangely vertical. We twiddle the dials and walk around the bodies. Sturdy, well-thought-of, wealthy and famous names. We shoppers are anonymous.

A woman in a tweed coat tries to get a picture on one of the plugged-in TV's. A salesman strolls over, calling out as he approaches: "What are you fiddling, lady? What are you trying to get here? San Francisco? It's a television set. With a few channels. With twenty-one-inch screen. With indoor antennae. With walnut cabinet. It's all written on the card here."

"Why does it get such a blurry picture?"

The salesman tilts his head back and closes his eyes. When he recovers he asks, "What are we, babies? In a store full of electrical equipment and all kinds of static interference you expect to get a picture like you would in your home?"

"Then why have it plugged in? People are supposed to try it, aren't they?"

"There's nothing to try. There's nothing to *try!*" He bangs the cabinet with the flat of his hand. "This here's a Zenith! You know what that name means. A Zenith. You've seen a hundred ads. What paper do you read, the *News?* It's in the *News.* What magazine do you read? *Screen Romance?* It's in that, too. You want to watch a Western? It won't cross you up and make you look at the Philharmonic."

"You don't know what I read," the woman says angrily. "You don't know what I watch."

"I don't wanna know."

"You're very fresh."

"I'm sorry!" the salesman shouts.

The woman walks deeper into the forest of sets. She takes off her wet tweed coat and carries it on her arm. She goes on twiddling the knobs and telescoping the antennae up and down. Even on the sets that are not plugged in. She walks back to the salesman.

"Is that one a good set?" She points. Her voice and expression are the same as at first, as if there had been no exchange of "You're very fresh" and the yelled "I'm sorry."

"It's an RCA." The salesman also is neutral and stolid. "You know the reputation of the RCA."

"But which one is better?"

"They're all good. All good. You pick the one you want and the store takes your money."

"But one set has got to be better than the other. The dark brown one is fifteen dollars more than the light brown. Doesn't that mean it's a better set?"

"You want me to talk you in? You want me to sell you, is that it? I'll tell you what you do. You go over to B. Altman's on Fifth Avenue. Walk into the radio department. Pick yourself a salesman, let him demonstrate all the pieces. Then when you decide what you want, you can come back here."

The woman looks at the forest of boxes, undecided.

"Unless you want to pick one out right now. While we have them on the floor."

"Why? Are you expecting any trouble ordering them?"

"I couldn't promise anything one day to the next. Right now the sets are here on the floor. Who knows about tomorrow?"

"I wouldn't decide without my husband, anyway," the woman remembers to say.

"Perfectly all right," the salesman says bitterly. "I knew

you were just shopping around." He pulls out his card. "When you're ready to buy, you come back and ask for me."

I watch the woman walk toward the elevators. The card floats from her hand as she steps in.

Stanwood has finished with his customer, but now the other salesman intercepts him before I can catch his attention.

"You saw me, how I handled that, was I right?" he asks Stanwood. "You gotta be tough with them, Stan, or they'll murder your time. There's something about bargain hunters. They're greedy. Present company excluded, miss. I don't care for them, frankly. This woman'll go to three other discount houses and spend two bucks in carfare to slice off another nickel. I don't know. I been working here ten years. There's something about the element that comes into a discount house, what is it?"

Stanwood shakes his head and shrugs.

"You don't want to do nothing for them," the other man goes on. "You want to give them a kick in the ass. Go on, you slobs, you feel like saying. You know what I mean?"

"I'm a miser myself," Stanwood says.

"No, I got sympathy for the people who want bargains." A third salesman has joined them. A slight red-haired man who has strolled, dwarfed by the big machines, from the home-appliance area.

"They don't just look to save money," he says. "That's only the first thing. Every penny they save, that's another penny toward the kids' education or a vacation, or maybe just plain food. But on top of that, it's also the feeling, the *feeling*, you know that feeling that for once these big companies are not taking you for a ride. Sure, they fix the prices. They fix them and fix them. We can only give a discount on the price they fix. But at least it's a little bit less. You don't have to walk in like a dummy and pay the price on the tag and thanks for nothing. You get a little bit, a little bit—" he moves his arm, palm up, fingers curling in a surreptitious summoning motion—"a little bit you steal back. A little bit of your own. I don't know. Somehow, to me, that's what a bargain is. And I got sympathy for these people. If I'm not busy, I answer their questions. What does it hurt me? Which machine is the bargain? This machine is the bargain. Because it'll last longer. But this one'll hold more clothes. This one will dry you faster. Which one is worth the price? Nothing is worth the price. The price is dictated to us. But you can save a little here and stretch a little on the other. You see, Stan?"

"I'm a miser myself. So I sympathize."

"Not misers." The little man grows restless and fidgety. "No misers. They want to save from one thing so they'll have for the other. See the difference?"

"I'm the same," Stanwood says.

Everybody shrugs. The group breaks up. Stanwood turns and sees me. "Jean!" He kisses me on the cheek. "Anything wrong at home?"

"Quick! Sell me a radio before they go out of stock."

While I wait for my deluxe model FM-AM, clock radio and plug-in coffee percolator to be wrapped, Stanwood suggests, since he has the early lunch shift today, that we leave together.

"I ought to be ashamed to let you see how miserly I eat," Stanwood says. "But if you can stand it I'd love your company."

"I lived on this stuff when I first came to New York," I

157

tell him while we are standing at the stand-up counter, eating our franks and relish and drinking our watery fruit drinks.

Near us stand four or five ragged Negro children, eating their frankfurters seriously, watching the skinny franks in their rolls as if they might disappear too fast. Their perfect brown fingers clutch their rolls two-handed.

Stanwood looks away into the thin drizzle that is still falling.

"We ought not to let these things affect us," he says.

"I suppose."

"A certain amount of toughness belongs in the human heart, that's it. If you weep for every passing pity, what's left?" He chews angrily. "What's left for Lillian?"

"Lillian?"

"I tell myself, Jean, that I'm not going to let myself be a damn dupe of feelings that have no place in the human heart." He belches and thumps at his chest. "Damn it! What's left for Lillian!"

I eat. The colored kids eat.

"I remind myself," he says, "many good men in history have not been humane. They have been good in the things they were good in. Bravery, loyalty to their own group, sometimes even kindness for aged parents thrown in. They never let themselves be melted down by pity for people they never met. A mistake. A bad mutation of human feeling."

"I think I'm going to have a powdered doughnut for dessert," I say.

"Let's make it two."

We have each saved an inch of our drink for the doughnut.

"I'd like very much to tell you something, Jean."

"Why don't you then?"

"I won't do it. Hattie fills you full enough."

"I could probably squeeze in a little more."

"No. Not today. Maybe sometime. . . ."

A Negro mother with a blanket-covered baby in her arms and a small waddling boy beside her, wipes her mouth and then her son's, and takes her family out into the drizzle. In the street she stops her son with a shake at his arm and looks critically at him. He is stock-still in his dark blue snowsuit. His bundled arms stick out like penguin flippers. His brown leather helmet, round and hard as half a volley ball, has flaps that also stick straight out. It is as if, rooted and fearful as he is, with his fat brown face lifted straight up in the rain to his mother, he is also miraculously winged. The helmet does not sit right. Brown as the helmet is, dark brown as the face, it seems to want to rise up from the brown head with a slow puffing up of air. The mother tugs at the right flap. We can see the bundled body tip over with the tug. Then she tugs the left side. The blue snowsuit bundle dips that way. The fat little brown mother-watcher has enough of dipping and lets out a quick squawk. Mother raps with backs of fingers like a knock at a door on the wide face.

"You mind me, Eustace!"

New, unthought-of attention. Up, up, the wide face looks. Eustace stands, arms and ear flaps akimbo, like a small penguin in the rain, his face turned up to her as to God, to take away the wet, to give him something from the package, to bring them safely home, to show him, after three or four hours of frowns and raps and commands, a smile that would set his solemn little body free.

"Son of a bitch," Stanwood says. "Not a face does that Ezra get. He's out there with five cameras and pouches bursting with film. What a waste of skill and knowledge. Not a face . . ."

"I'm getting a heartburn hangover from this so-called food," I say. "Let's get away from the smell at least."

We draw each other away, both of us suppressing belches. Stanwood puts his hand over his chest and rubs it. "What a mistake to weep for every passing pity," he says softly. "God help us all. God help Lillian."

Twenty-two

It is midnight. Jesús' hour. Feed him a steak, let him shower and get into bed and hold him and Go-Man-Go and then, before his eyelids have quite fluttered closed, "You want to hear some more of the story, Jesús?"

"I don' know. You got much more of that stuff?"

"Don't you like it?"

"I don' know if I like it or what. But I never heard nothin' like that before."

"Okay. So you're learning something new, right?"

"Yeah, I suppose you could say that. What is it, anyhow?"

"It's biography, the story of somebody's life. It's an American life."

"Yeah—well, but a girl's life."

"Okay—here's something from a boy's life."

I read:

Standing in his father's living-room, Ezra shifted his straps and pouches, heavily weighted. He stared down at the oval rug his mother had worked from bright patches, while his father looked with interest at his own feet, soak-ing in an enamel basin of water.

"*I suppose you're mad about it just on general princi-ples,*" Ezra told his father, to provoke him a little. Other-wise there might be nothing. "*Just because it's something I'm doing.*"

"*Why the hell should that bother me? Do you think I give a damn? You're not the first fella that's made this particular mistake.*"

"*Why has it got to be a mistake?*" Ezra said. His equip-ment, which he always made a point of wearing when he spoke to his father ("*like armor,*" he thought of it to him-self) weighed as heavily as an animal carcass on his back. "*Hattie's a fine girl.*"

"*That so?*" his father said, twitching his toes in the water. "*Well, I hope she's a good worker, too, so's she can pay for some of that armor you're always buying.*"

The fact that his father had the same image of his equip-ment as he did startled him, but it shouldn't have. His fa-ther and mother had also been enemies, and he often had proof that the same sour thoughts ran through both their heads. Close was close. And kept married people together till they died.

"*She's up at the college,*" Ezra said. "*She'll be finished in May, and we're not waiting for the graduation exer-cises.*"

His father stamped both feet in the basin, and little waves of water leaped over the basin's rim to the floor. He twisted his stout body around so he could see Ezra better, leaning on the bathrobe-wrapped knees.

"*At the college! Don't tell me you had the sense . . . !*

By God—" he smiled his brown-toothed, terrifying smile at his son—"you've got yourself a rich one!"

"She's no richer than we are."

"Well, it's very nice of you to have that free and equal opinion of your own family." His father sank his round chin into his neck and looked wickedly solemn. "Very respectful. Good boy." Then his ugly brown teeth began to peep from the reddish mustache again and his face grew florid as he shouted, "But it's damn few daughters of any family would be up at the college on no richer than we are!"

Ezra waited while his father's face sank into that puffed, yet at the same time pinched look. As if he puffed himself up the way certain small animals did in order to conceal helplessness from his enemies. If his father could have shot out black ink, Ezra felt, or a sharp quill, or a huge bad smell, he would have. His father had never beaten him as a boy or struck his mother or any man, as far as he knew. But his own beaten look had venom in it. As if his father wanted to say, "Here, this is how bad things are with me. And you can blacken in my blot, and prick with my stick and stink up in my stench. You bastard. You walked one step too close to a suffering man."

Ezra kept his eyes on his father, who was watching his own feet. While he waited, he quietly absorbed his dose of ink, sticker and smell. The doses had gotten smaller than the overwhelming ones that had squirted out at him as a boy, leaving him almost mad with bafflement as to what it could all mean. Now he knew it was terror in its turn—envy, despair, longing, cursing and other natural things —as familiar to his camera world as balustrades and windows.

After a while he said quietly, "No, she's a poor girl."

His father looked up with a bright animal expression, full of curiosity, as if he'd forgotten why he was puffed, or what was threatening him. He twitched his reddish mustache hairs inquisitively. "What, has she got rich aunties, then?" he wondered in a plain, reasonable voice.

Suddenly the fox was loose again and he turned, quick and nimble.

"O ho!" Nimble as a fox and barking like a seal. "A scholarship kid! O Jesus, Jesus!" He paddled his big white feet in the water and laughed with all his brown teeth showing. He was a jolly laugher, a good choice for campus watchman, round and merry and redhaired, with blue eyes that watered, and a great favorite for the "Good evenings," and "Good mornings, Mr. Zindler," with the teachers and the girls. Only the tarred teeth to Ezra showed the bitter turn of the tide.

"Christ!" His father slapped his legs and laughed a bad smell from his mouth and shot his arm out to point at Ezra.

"You booby! You managed to hook a girl from one of the richest colleges in the country. But she's a scholarship girl. Christ!" A new thought within a thought struck him and his laugh sputtered out again; his voice got louder. "You looked real good through your lenses and your light meters—" (heff, heff, like a walrus barking)—"and you found her. That shows you—" he was snared in the discovery and could hardly catch his breath, hurling himself around inside the snare like an animal—"how people are made."

All at once he was calm, and was patting his big pale feet dry with a towel. "It's a perfect example of fate." Patting the sensitive soles and in between the toes. "If a man crosses a desert and drowns in the only waterhole there is, you got to call that fate. And if a poor man's son gets into a rich girls' college and marries one poor girl out of the thousand rich ones that are there—" He stepped onto the towel and looked down at his clean feet.

Ezra had periodically, from boyhood on, longed to beat his father. To pound that dense head of which the falsely smiling face was so small a part, like a round, bald paperweight on which a blurred design of features was stenciled near the bottom. The equipment was not only armor. It was weapons, too. Not the Leicas and Rolleis. They would themselves be injured. But in the bulging leather pouch he carried film frames, heavy iron squares, soldered at the corners. "Pow-wow-wow!" He could have beaten him. And the heavy frames would make a deceptively light sound as the thin metal-sheet-backing rattled.

"You money-glut bastard!" Ezra said, though that was not what he hated his father for. He said it in a controlled voice, his hand tightening on the leather strap and pulling the equipment pouch forward over his hip.

"Yes, I am naughty, amn't I?" his father sneered. As if to say—but then, in a minute, he said it: "The ladies up at school wouldn't care for me if they knew, would they?"

Ezra gave his leather bag a push backward and the heavy weight of it fell against his back, a familiar goad.

"I'll be moving away soon to New York. We won't see each other any more. And that's fate, too. You were the hole in this desert that nearly drowned me. And I'm moving now, I'm not waiting."

"Shacking up with your slut? Good! And when you get to New York, give my love to the Jews."

165

"You lousy fraud! You have no love. Your soul is Nazi!" Wham! He kicked the basin into the air and the water fell first, collapsing like a rope ladder, and then the basin bounced—side, handle and clop! empty mouth down.

"I always knew you!" he yelled. "Through and through! But you made me suffer. When I was little I suffered, because I wasn't sure and you sometimes smiled at me!" He shook his fist. "No more smiles, enemy!"

He whirled to walk out and the heavy pouch slammed him on the back. As he grabbed the two bags from the porch in both hands and ran down the steps, he felt sick. Not so much from the heart-pumping quarrel as from the remorse that caught him in that last look at the room as he turned. His father, who loved to be clean, had stood looking down at his feet over which the dirty water had tumbled. And Ezra, for a confused moment, had felt what he would have felt as a small boy—the sin of what he had done. He walked quickly the twelve blocks to Stanwood's house, never stopping to change hands, as if he carried nothing heavier than his rage.

"What do you think of this father, Jesús?"

Jesús slams his fist into the pillow.

"Motherin' bastards! You got to kill them fathers before they kill you!" he shouts.

Mario falls with a terrible thud from his bed.

Jesús is crying.

"Ssh. Don't, don't. Listen, the person who wrote this about the boy and his father wrote something about it afterward. Something she understood about it. Listen, Jesús!"

I read, my arms around Jesús and Hattie's manuscript

propped on the pillow above his head, from Hattie's post-script.

You see, Jean, I understand what made Ezra Ezra. People who were loved badly at the beginning fear love later. These are the ordinary *terrors of being alive. Sisyphus—rolling the stone endlessly up the mountain—is the symbol for man. Excruciating enough, isn't it? This picture of someone struggling all his life to do the undoable? But that's just ordinary life. Everybody's task. For a man to become a man after his father unmanned him. To become loving although no one loved him. Ordinary tasks . . . .*

I look sideways at Jesús. His mouth gapes open, the tears hang on his cheeks.

That's what it is. All Ezra's troubles and mine, Lillian's, Stanwood's, yours, Sostana's, everyone's—that's just the ordinary pushing up the mountain. Some of us get smashed from our own efforts. . . .

"Tha's right," Jesús whispers. "Some of us get smashed. . . ."

Now suppose this. While Sisyphus keeps pushing that boulder up the mountain and never making it, another boulder, from somewhere out there, comes hurtling down and smashes him. This smashing from the outside—this power of evil we're learning about now that smashes down on us, this knowing of it, touching it, then I don't know what—it turns me to jelly.

✓ ✓ ✓

"Wha's it sayin' there?" Jesús asks.

"She means a man called Hitler. He was very powerful for a while, and evil."

"I like to read abou' *that* guy!"

Twenty-three |

I am up most of the night now reading mystery stories. I sleep through most of the morning. When I wake up I run down for the mail and scratch through it like a starving dog. Loftus, I'm bitching. Can you hear me?

I drink black coffee and read the foursome's lives, embellished by Hattie's literary flourishes. On my own part it's literary Peeping Tomism. My own life is suspended, so I live in Hattie's and the foursome's.

My layouts are late. There are calls from art editors wanting to know about them. I hate to go out, for fear you'll call then. But when the phone rings it's either an editor reminding me of his schedule or Hattie reminding me of hers.

Aside from Sostana, I see Hattie and the foursome. Jesús slips in and out.

Twenty-four |

"Here's more, Jesús. More American biography. Listen."

By the next night I have managed to hunt up Hattie's account of how the foursome found their apartments. I want to read it to Jesús in case he still feels resentful about the apartment situation. We still look at apartments for Jesús from time to time, but nothing I can afford appeals to him. Nothing reminds him enough of my place.

"Listen! 'How We Came to New York. Part One: Ezra and Stanwood.' "

"Who's that again?" Jesús asks, very bored.

"It doesn't matter—they could be anybody."

"Ezra—he that guy with the father?"

"That's right."

"Okay." Jesús settles himself against the pillow, his naked, narrow chest shiny with bones.

Ezra and Stanwood rode the train to New York to find, in one weekend, two apartments that would suit the two couples.

While they were on the train, Ezra looked through the window at the black verticals of telephone poles that rose like winter trees from the spring-yellowing earth. "Steichen did a beautiful series of this," he told Stanwood. "Nobody should ever touch something any more that's been done wonderfully."

They picked the East Side of Manhattan because the buildings excited Ezra. "They're all different sizes here," he pointed out to Stanwood. "You get angles and contrasts and shadows thrown down from the big ones onto the little ones. See?"

He pointed to a sparkling three-story mansion made of large whitish blocks of stone into which one shoulder of the adjacent white-brick terraced apartment house cut a wedge of shadow.

That was on Fifth Avenue. It was Sunday, and they were walking east to the rising sun because the competition would be fierce. They wanted to avoid paying an agent's fee. Their only hope, if there was anything suitable, was to get there first.

Stanwood had to prod Ezra to keep moving. If they found two apartments in a rent-controlled house it would be a miracle; if they found one they would share it; if they found nothing, they would have to come back and start again.

Ezra went a little mad on Park Avenue. The almost square, huge-stoned houses with the widely spaced casement windows reminded him of some ancient Italian palazzos he had seen in an architectural magazine. He would have liked to do a series on these stone façades. The patterns of stone and glass gave great serenity. He had to stop for a picture.

"I know it's been done." He grinned apologetically at Stanwood. "This is for myself."

As they walked up the side streets under the bare, snub-budded ginkgoes, they passed the brownstones and town houses with Victorian wrought-iron gates and stone grape arbors and black wood fanlight doors and brass lamps.

Ezra kept his broad fingers on his Leica, but did not snap. Stanwood saw him staring from house to house and knew that for him it was the same as reading a book, and didn't interrupt him.

"I won't do these," Ezra was saying, as if to himself. "They're almost too quaint, too cute. Aside from their having been done, too. I like more massiveness. More solid, heavy stuff."

He glanced back toward Park, and for a while walked backward, squinting up the street toward the big buildings they had left. Stanwood turned him around after a while. "We'd better get there, Ez."

When they got to the apartment house where "several choice apartments for the right parties" were advertised, they were late, they found. The sun was still low, the street was quiet. But already a small stream of people was heading into the building, number 343. These applicants walked quickly, with newspapers tucked under their arms. They kept their eyes down and hurried as if afraid to see the other people hurrying to the same destination. One young man held a two-year-old child on his shoulder and didn't wait for the elevator. He ran up the stairs two at a time.

After Ezra and Stanwood looked around the lobby— stripped bare of everything except a brown chandelier with tiny bulbs giving off a brown light—they stepped out onto the sidewalk again.

"Not much use," Ezra said. "But look."

He pointed across the street, where there were two small stone houses side by side in a row of similar ones, going up the inclining hill of the street. On one a wisteria vine climbed from a two-by-four plot of dirt next to the door. On the next house gray streamers of pigeon drop striped the façade.

Ezra took a picture of that. Of the flowers climbing up one wall and the excrement sliding down the other.

"Nothing special," he said. "A little visual joke." He tried to sound casual, but Stanwood could see how excited he was. He changed rolls quickly and pushed the little wound-up roll in his bulging pack.

"Good haul," Stanwood said. "All that's missing is an apartment for us."

"Just a lot of little things." Ezra grinned apologetically, but his hands were shaking with excitement.

"I like this neighborhood, Stan. I like this street. I like this house. What a shame we're too late."

They stood, undecided, watching new people hurry in.

"I don't see the same people who went in rushing out again. Looks like there's something doing inside when they get there," Stanwood said.

"Maybe there's more than one apartment," Ezra said. "Maybe the whole building is full of apartments to rent."

"Maybe it's not just who's first. Maybe there are other things involved."

They were slowly nudging each other toward the entrance. They walked through the glass doors and up the three low marble steps inside the lobby.

"Maybe the landlord," Ezra said, "is from a small town

*and is looking to do a good turn to people in the same situa-
tion."*

*They began to hurry toward the elevator, hardly taking
in the almost bare lobby, whose only furniture was a large
stone urn set in a wall niche.*

*As the elevator sprang open, a knot of people hurried
out. The young man with the little boy on his shoulder
was first, taking big long-legged steps, running down toward the three steps. Two young women hurrying after
looked angry. A couple was last. The young man, seeing
the folded newspaper under Stanwood's arm said, "Save
yourself a trip. The old bastard's gone nuts on power. He
won't rent. He's having too much fun torturing people."*

*Ezra and Stanwood stepped into the self-service eleva-
tor, also brown. Names scratched into the dark varnish.*

*Ezra, biting his lower lip and laughing at his own ex-
citement said, "I've got my dragon film ready."*

*· They got off at the fifth floor and went, following the
sound of angry voices, toward the open apartment door at
the end of the hall.*

*An old man, wearing sunglasses, stood with his back to
a window, right forefinger upraised at the people grouped
in front of him.*

*"Only one person at a time," he said with dragging slow-
ness. "I am only the renting agent."*

*If he was enjoying holding these people at bay, his face
didn't show it. It was creased and heavy with concern. He
scratched at his forehead under his loud plaid cap, plunged
his hands into first one, then the other of the loaded pockets of his sagging green hound's-tooth jacket. Then he dug
his hands into the pockets of his broad brown pants. From*

all the pockets he extracted small slips of paper, written on, folded and smeared.

"Did I get your name here?" he asked a man up front, in a worried voice.

"You got all our names. Three days ago. When are you gonna decide, mister?"

The renting agent looked up severely over the rims of his sunglasses. "You could go home," he said to the man who had spoken.

"What did I say?"

"It's what I said. You can go home. I can't use you and my building can't use you."

"I thought you said you were the agent."

"I am the agent. And you could go home."

"Look, sir," another voice said with exaggerated politeness. "It's already the fifth of the month. Surely the owner of the building would like to start collecting rent. What's the good of keeping those two apartments empty?"

Stanwood and Ezra nudged each other. Two.

"Don't worry," another voice said bitterly. "They'll wait till the fifteenth of the month and they'll still charge you from the first. They won't lose out."

A pretty, well-dressed young woman said sweetly, "I will pay you from the first, gladly."

"No single girls," the agent growled. He addressed the others. "She'll take in four roommates, three will get married, the fourth will sublet. How can I keep track of the caliber? Who is responsible, hah? Go home to Mama!"

"I left my mama a long time ago," the girl said fiercely.

"You should write her a nice letter and then go home to her," the agent said. "I don't want no baby dolls in my house."

"You're some agent!"

The man shook a finger. "Insults! True colors!" After a minute he added in an offended voice, "It's for the good of the tenant, whoever he will be, that I'm checking up on everybody. Do you care who is your neighbor? Do you want to move in with any filth that wants to live next to you?"

There was a chorus of: "I need the apartment. Let me worry about that," and so on.

The agent shook his head. "I will not be rushed. And if this bunch don't work out I will put another ad in the paper and interview some more."

A man who had been standing near the front suddenly twitched around and shoved out. "Go to hell, you bastard!" He was followed by several others who went, cursing.

The agent stamped his foot. "Weeding out. This is what I want to see. True character. Who will be what kind of tenant. I want for my tenants—is it so terrible?—ladies and gentlemen. Where can an agent find any more ladies and gentlemen?"

He looked at Ezra and Stanwood. "Who sent you?"

Stanwood took half a step forward. "We saw your ad. We are in New York only for the weekend . . ."

"From where?"

"From Massachusetts, where we live now. But we're very anxious to move to New York, and need two apartments . . ."

"Massachusetts where?"

"A very small town. So small you probably haven't even heard of it."

"*I haven't? Why two apartments? Don't you like each other?*"

"*We're both married.*"

"*Any children?*"

"*Not—yet.*"

"*I am not against children. I like substantial family people.*" *He turned to Ezra.* "*What is your work?*"

"*I'm a photographer.*"

The agent took a step backward. "*What, an artist?*"

Ezra considered. "*No,*" *he answered steadily.* "*Not what you're afraid of. I'm a professional photographer.*"

"*You don't know what I'm afraid of,*" *the agent said.* "*I am afraid of riffraff. They will do any damage they please with your property. I don't go for this furnished-apartment business and you rent to any riffraff and you don't care who lives in your house till somebody buys it for a speculation. I want responsible people. Can you pay the rent?*"

"*Of course we can. How much is it?*"

"*We'll discuss that later. You want to look around?*"

They walked through the rooms. They were small but they were light, and the bedroom was a corner room with one window overlooking a garden next door.

Ezra and Stanwood nodded at each other.

"*You like it,*" *the agent said.* "*Good. This is not the apartment for rent. But the others are nice, too. One is bigger, one is smaller. Is that what you want?*"

"*That would be okay. If we can see them.*"

"*You can't. They are occupied.*"

"*Then what's for rent?*"

"*Them two I told you. When the time comes they will be empty.*"

"How?"

"Don't worry about my business, please. When the agreement is reached there will be no trouble about you moving in."

"Then we have the two apartments?"

"No," the agent said.

"We came a long way to find apartments," Stanwood said. "We hate to go back to our wives with no good news."

"That's it," the agent said. "The wives. I got to meet them."

"Man, them landlords!" Jesús bursts out. "They got too much power."

"You see!" I tell Jesús (I knew you was a teacher). "You're getting information. In other words, an education. It helps you to know how to look at things in the world."

"Go ahead," Jesús says. "Read more."

"This part is Hattie and Lillian."

"Who's that?"

"It doesn't matter. Girls."

"Go ahead. I'm gettin' sleepy."

Hattie and Lillian started at Broadway and Seventy-second Street, so their layer cake was not like Ezra's and Stanwood's, who began with Central Park, like a pretty frosting, and then walked layer by layer to First Avenue, the hard bottom crust.

Dutifully Hattie tried to admire the buildings, as Ezra had told her to do. They seemed closed and silent to her. Mammoth, aloof and hard. The people who walked the avenues seemed tiny. But as if to make up for that, the women enlarged themselves with thick fur coats, large fur hats, spike heels and platformed soles and carried enormous pocketbooks with big metal clasps.

The doorways of the houses on the East Side, like tiny mouths in vast faces, also tried to enlarge themselves with canopies, sidewalk runners, and sometimes with some kind of stiffly tied dark drapery on either flank.

As they approached the house where they expected to find the agent, Lillian said, "What could possibly go wrong?"

Stanwood had warned them, "He's touchy. He has a vision of the good. All of a sudden, since the apartment shortage, he has something rare in his hands—empty apartments—and he's in a position to bind and to loosen. He can reward the deserving and withhold from the undeserving —he thinks."

When Hattie and Lillian got to the house, the agent was standing in more or less the same spot in which Ezra and Stanwood had first seen him. The room was empty but for him. One foot, in its cracked brown shoe, rested on the ribs of the radiator. The agent was staring thoughtfully into space.

"We're the wives," Lillian began timidly. But still and all, speaking up.

"Put down, put down," the agent said wearily, "your names."

They wrote their names on the long sheet of yellow-pad paper, ruled with horizontal green lines.

The agent studied their names.

"I also need your references and where you work. But I tell you right now the corporation don't favor single girls

*young enough to marry. Older single girls wouldn't be
too bad. Also Lesbians, God forbid! are as substantial as
married people."*

"We're married," Lillian said. "You met our husbands."

*The agent stared at them and then glanced at his list.
"You are from a town in Massachusetts so small I never
heard of it. What is the name of that town?"*

"Fairmont," Lillian said.

*The agent tilted his head to one side and listened to its
echo. "You're right, I never heard of it."*

*"You told our husbands you wanted to meet us," Lillian
said. "We made the trip especially so you could see us."*

The agent looked at them and nodded without comment. "What work does your husband do?" he asked Lillian.

"He's a salesman."

"Your husband?" he asked Hattie.

"My husband is a photographer."

*"What about me?" A thickset, dark man emerged from
another room and strode into this one. He struck his fist
against his jacket. "You as good as promised me that apartment."*

*"As good as promised is your opinion. I reserve the right
to pick whoever I like for a tenant."*

*"You're torturing me! And I got a wife and four kids.
In two months they'll have no roof over their heads because the building's condemned!"*

*"Why are you torturing him?" Hattie demanded, taking
the man's side at once.*

*"Why did he wait till the last minute?" the agent shot
back. "You know what type he is? He don't care for his*

wife and his children. He drinks up half of what he earns and lets his children go hungry. When the kids cry he blames his boss, and when his family goes out on the street, he'll blame me. That's the type he is!" The agent was shouting, his cap pushed back on his head, and wagging his fist. "I investigated you!"

The leather-jacketed man covered his face with his hands. But only for a second. The next second his face was uncovered and he was shouting again, "You're torturing me!"

Then Hattie heard the sound that at that time was still strange to her, but which was to become familiar later, when they were finally settled in New York. It was an almost soundless preamble to what always followed, but it was the preamble itself that induced the heart-stopping fear.

The shoes did a fast-slow shuffle, heavy under the almost rigid body (there were even, when Hattie looked later, the dirt marks of heel scuffs against the baseboard of the wall behind the leather-jacketed man) and the sounds of that incredibly quick, clumsy, purposeful shuffle. Those were the sounds men made before they started to fight.

The next minute the leather-jacketed man threw himself forward and pounced, like a trapeze artist grabbing for the bar in mid-air, on the shoulders of the baggy-suited, rubber-kneed agent. When the agent was on his back, the leather-jacketed man proceeded both to choke and to bounce the agent's head on the old, sloping wooden floor. Neither uttered a sound.

"Ooooooh!" Lillian shrieked. "Let him go. Let him go. Let him go."

She tugged one arm and Hattie, sick as if seeing an accident in the street, tugged on the other.

The agent's head had stopped bouncing, but he glared, with the other man's hands around his neck, straight into the eyes of the other man.

"O let him go," Lillian coaxed. "Please, what can you gain? You'll find another apartment. He didn't mean that. Just walk away. Just let it go."

And that was what the man did. He got up, dusted his knees, wiped his palms, as if revolted, along his trouser legs, and walked away. He went through the empty rooms, out of the door and then they could hear him, not even waiting for the elevator, but running down the stairs.

On his back, from the floor, the agent said, "I give you the two apartments. Not for you—" he raised a dirt-tipped thumb to Hattie—"you are half-baked and a troublemaker. For you." He nodded at Lillian. "You got a good heart and maybe you could teach your sister something about life. Send me your husbands. And now go away. I don't need—" he pushed at Lillian's hand—"a doctor. Don't bring me any water. Just let me take a little rest."

He pushed his plaid cap over his face and for all they knew he was asleep on the floor as they, trembling and clutching hands, tiptoed out.

Lillian revived first. She began to recite, patting Hattie's arm as they walked along the street, "Greenwich Village and the Italian section, where they still play boccie, and the Lower East Side and Harlem and the Puerto Ricans in the melting pot. The museums. The UN, Hattie, how wonderful it will be for Ezra—and for the children. . . ."

✓ ✓ ✓

I turn to Jesús for his comment, but he is deeply asleep. And probably has been for some time. I'm sorry if he missed the part where the man with the leather jacket choked the agent. It would probably have been a relief for him to hear that.

It is very late when I finally get to sleep myself, my head full of apartments and renting agents. Just before waking, I see the apartment I want for Jesús, though I'm unable to locate it in any exact spot in the city.

It is one large room and very sunny, even though it is in the back—I suppose it's in the back, because it overlooks a garden. A studio bed against one wall is covered in blue —Jesús' favorite color—and there are beige linen curtains which filter light and throw soft, moving patterns against the creamy walls. The rest of the room is a study. Bookshelves everywhere, filled with books, and a big desk with a good light on it and a globe—"This is the world, Jesús" —and prints of Picasso and Rivera and Orozco.

I don't dare tell Jesús about it. He leaves after breakfast with his ten dollars, and not a word more said about apartments

Twenty-five |

Sostana comes down for an evening drink.

"I'll tell you what about children. Here is a story, eh?
Dio! How much weeping one could do for women. But it's
no use, so one laughs instead. That is really much better.
They deserve what they get, don't they really?

"But listen. Once a woman worked for me. A lovely
young black woman from the Indies. She earned a bit of
money cleaning my apartment and she earned a bit cleaning someone else's. She was going to school. To become
just what I forget. Some kind of hospital thing. An aide, a
practical nurse, maybe.

"She had already taken up in her hands all the torn edges
of her life and had somehow tucked them back in. She had
had an illegitimate child when she was fifteen. Her husband
let the boy come and live with them when they moved to
the States. She had sweated through all that business of five
children in three rooms and finally they were all of them
of school age and going to their school in Harlem. She had
them all *going*, too. Clean and nice and reading and learning. And she was going to school, too, you see? I remem-

ber how she said in such a delightful, laughing voice, 'School is a blessed place to send them through the door.'

"Then one day at five o'clock as she was leaving my apartment she folded her hands together and told me, 'I believe that children are from God. So I cannot be sorry I am pregnant again.'

"When she left she told me that by the time her baby was old enough to go to school she would be past the age limit for the hospital training program she had counted on.

"I missed her when she left because we used to tell each other things I don't think we told other people. Like when she told me about the first child. She said, 'My mother said it was a thing that could happen to anybody.' She put all that trust in me right at the beginning, eh? You see she was saying to me, 'This is how you are to see me. As my mother did.' But, of course, I did see her that way. I was convinced—you see?—she would keep on picking up the pieces with her two hands until she had put her life and the life of her family into some good shape. And she believed the same thing of me. Do you see that? She said to me, 'You will rise up. I can see that in you.' *Dio!* It's better to laugh!

"How we talked! Like midwives! Episiotomies and hemorrhages and breech births and black labors that made you climb the walls of a room. She told me, 'I am an old soldier in these wars.' She had to have her babies in the ward, where they always sent the greenest interns to poke around and see what they could learn. Once she told a little blond one with skinny fingers, 'My case is not for you, little boy, you had better go home.'

"We laughed. O *Dio!* how we laughed!

"I didn't see her again for a long time. Then one day I

was standing on the subway platform waiting for a downtown train and I heard a woman near me say to her friend,
'Now I've seen everything!' I turned around to where she
was showing her friend, eh? I saw a woman coming down
the steps on the uptown side. There were three children
hanging on to her dress, looking scared, while she bumped
a yelling baby in an open stroller down the steps. It took me
a while to recognize her, you see. She wore those cheap,
sharpie shoes with pointed toes and all turned over with
heavy walking. Her dress was an old maternity one with
strings hanging from the middle, and the seam was giving
where the kids pulled. Her hair seemed to be actually jump-
ing into points from her head. But most of all it was, *Dio!*,
the look on her face. She had always been humorous and
slow. But now she was cuffing the kids and pulling at them.
Her face looked wicked.

"I moved away, so she wouldn't have to see me. But I
was thinking, it's happened. This time she won't put the
pieces together again.

"A woman falls from her class down to the lower one
faster than a man ever can. And the reason is, my dear,
children. . . ."

Sostana raises her glass. But I can't be sure whether it's
to me or to Mario, thumping over our heads.

Twenty-six |

I am so wary of the mailbox that I have taken to letting it go unchecked till evening, or even skipping whole days. Now I see your letter has lain there since yesterday.

"My darling Jean—

"Thank God I am not with you now. I feel covered with the slime of my own existence. We are not letting ourselves off easily, Erna and I.

"We are not letting ourselves off easily . . . don't think that . . . our talks are terrible . . . Erna talks, I talk . . . we can't stop talking now . . . everything comes out . . . every disappointment . . . every betrayal . . . from the joint bank account to the marriage bed. . . .

"We are both exhausted. We are going into material we never could touch before. It's strange. Delving—even into painful material—gives that material an aliveness. Years and years of my life—that I had thought too painful to think about, too stinkingly dead to dare touch, are beginning to throb and to take on a certain terrible vivacity.

Just think! It would all have been left in deadness. There would have been no enlightenment of those dark years, if suddenly Erna hadn't seen it was all going to be coffined and buried as was. Now she wants to wash and dress the body of defeated love.

"How much I'm learning about what I was in those years . . . more than I care to know . . . I'll be a better husband after all this . . . this therapy is long overdue . . . our last chance, as Erna says, to be honest with one another. . . . Be patient . . . if I can dispose of the garbage in my life now, you and I will be happier for it later. . . .

"Have I told you that your letters about Hattie and the foursome bring me to tears? (I have to admit, I am fairly easily brought to tears these days.) All those sweet sillinesses, those innocent vapidities you write me about. I go along with that horse's ass of an art editor. Blessings on the four. Blessings also on the two, on the one! God bless us all! I feel as maudlin as Tiny Tim. . . .

"My darling . . . I am so moved by the delicacy of your speaking to me through the lives of other people. In a way I feel I am speaking to you through Erna . . . do you feel how I am speaking to you through Erna . . . ?

"P.S. Your essayist who writes about joy—my God, yes! let's have joy! O but these philosophers with their exhortations. If ever there was one who could tell us how to get from where we are to where we want to be . . . !"

Twenty-seven |

"I got into some trouble, Jean," Jesús honorably declares before he even crosses my threshold.

I pull at his arm and draw him in and lock the door.

"What kind of trouble?"

"Me and a couple of my buddies was downtown. And these guys came by and one of them shoved one of my buddies. So my buddy took a swing at him and the other guy's buddies come in on top of him. So me and my other buddy come in on top of them. So two of the other guys they pulled knives."

"And?"

"And so one of the guys he got hurt."

"Stabbed?"

"Yeah."

"How badly?"

"Cut up pretty bad. He was layin' there in the gutter and he was bleedin'. He din' look like he could get up."

"O God, Jesús!"

"I din' even know this guy. I feel very bad, you know? I got nothin' against him, except I gotta defen' my buddy."

He looks directly at me and across his smooth face there moves a kind of anguish and he asks, "Is it still okay if I stay?"

"Yes. It's still okay."

In the morning, just before he leaves, he says, "I got to disappear for a while."

"Don't disappear, Jesús. You might not ever get found again."

"But I better not come back for a while. Some of my buddies know about this place."

"Would your buddies tell?"

"I don' think my buddies would tell. But if somebody get caught by the police, they might get very scare'."

I hesitate with my hand on my wallet. If I give him too much he may not come back. If too little, he may be lost. In the end I say, "Here is your usual allowance, Jesús. Come back."

Twenty-eight |

"Dear Loftus—

"I've been wanting to tell you this. I met a Puerto Rican boy who had no place to sleep and I told him he could come to my apartment any time he needed to. He came a few times. Then he got into a street fight and someone was hurt. I'm sure he's not the one who did the stabbing, but now he has stopped coming. I worry about him. Every time I hear a cat in the courtyard I think of Jesús. You know those dotty old women who go out in the rain to feed cats and pigeons? Could I get like that? Feeding skinny Puerto Rican boys in alleys?

"I don't understand anything about relationships. But anyway, I enclose Hattie's 'Evening Shopping.' I don't know whether I'm speaking to you through this one, or whether it's moving. It's just here, on top of my papers, and I don't know what else to do with it. . . ."

When she shopped late on Friday nights in the A & P, Hattie was able to see the women and their escorts headed for the night clubs in her neighborhood: El Morocco, the

Embers, La Zambra. Those were some of the places in New York that attracted out-of-towners hell-bent for fun in the city. The respectable men and women from Cleveland and Denver and Oklahoma City. The Elks and the Lions and their wives; the Shriners and Rotarians and their Rotary Ann's.

On those evenings Hattie had to carry out her shopping with bad thoughts which she tried hard to exorcise, lest they somehow take away from the nourishment of the food she bought.

She was the kind of woman who, when she made a shopping list, didn't just write down:

1 pound hamburger
2 cans tomato paste
1 quart milk
1 frozen peas.

Instead she wrote:

1 pound hamburger for Ezra and me
lamb chops for Lillian and Stan's dinner
tutti-frutti ice cream for all of us tonight

So that she was surrounded, when she shopped, even in the mob at the meat counter where there was a special on porterhouse, by people she loved.

When she shopped during the day, there were women who had small babies perched in the front seats of their shopping carts, surrounded by cans and boxes. The infants eyed the food that was piling up as possessively as if they intended, once they got home, to consume it all. Now and then the mother, adding a bright box of something would say, "See, these are for after lunch."

Hattie also felt as if her family's spirit were being

wheeled along in her cart. As she placed each item in her wire basket she said over to herself, "Tutti-frutti for all of us, lamb chops for them, milk for baby and me. . . ."
It made her exceedingly happy.

That was why, when she saw the women on their way, with escorts, to El Morocco, the Embers, La Zambra, she wished with all her heart for some voodoo magic, some amulet against the evil eye that would ward off from her food dryness and staleness and poison and worms. They frightened her, these women, and the fear might contaminate not only the baby inside her, but the crackers and powders and cheeses in the bright boxes.

These women wore tight dresses, often shiny—a satin or brocade. Then they wore a fur jacket on top, in which they huddled the top parts of themselves. They had the look of centaurs—developed and expanded at the top, and the haunches lean and powerful. On their feet they wore very high-heeled shoes and they took short, huddling steps, stamping at the ground whole hoofs at once, like stiff, pampered ponies. Their hair was always very blond or very black and set—carved into something hard and unbreakable.

They stood on the street corners, two or three women together, stamping their stiff shoes at the ground, while the men struck out into the gutters, throwing themselves into the paths of onrushing cars, waving madly for taxis. Sometimes the women screamed helpfully, "Here comes one—get that one!"

The devil was in their eyes. Whether they were stamp-stamping and huddling along the street, hanging from their escorts' arms, or screaming on a street corner, or laughing hard going in or coming out of El Morocco, the Embers,

La Zambra, when Hattie saw them it was always there. It wasn't a cunning devil. Not even a malicious one. But an absolutely selfish and uncaring devil who stamp-stamped over the world and everyone in it. Sometimes in this neighborhood there were drunks sleeping in the doorways of the Second Avenue tenements. There were no beggars dying in the streets, no little children sitting next to their mothers with rice bowls. But if there had been, those shiny women with their screaming laughs would have huddled and stamped their way past them, uncaring. That must be how it was in New Delhi, in Rome, in Paris, in Athens, and in the cities among the stars.

That's how it was, and it frightened Hattie. As she walked along with her shopping cart and her list she hummed to herself, to the tune of "There's a Hole in the Bottom of the Sea":

O I'm frightened of the evil in this world
I am frightened of the evil that is there
I am frightened
I am frightened
The evil in this world gives me a scare!

To calm herself, she murmured, "Yogurt for Stanwood, skimmed milk for Lillian, blue cheese for Ezra, tutti-frutti for all of us. . . ."

"P.S.: Lillian has confided to me that Hattie has confided to her that she is thinking of starting to write a novel. The subject is secret. Lillian is delighted. 'Hattie will have an interest,' Lillian says, 'till the baby comes. . . .' "

Twenty-nine |

The wall-thumpers are at it again.

"Everybody knowing everything about everyone else," Hattie says. "That's part of the trouble."

"That's supposed to make people strong," says Stanwood.

"Yes, but only if it doesn't kill them first. And with husband and wife—compounded a million times. The things you know about me, Ezra. The things I know about you. My husband's weakness and the world's iniquity—both exposed to me at the same time."

Broad smiles all round the foursome. The walls stand firm. They rest their smiles on me, too, for a minute—breathing easy, wall-like rhythms.

"Never mind the world's weakness," Ezra says, laughing. "What about the husband's iniquities?"

"Are you faithful to me?"

"In my fashion, love . . . "

"The things you correlate!" Stanwood takes up his turn at thumping. "Solipsism, Hattie. Lilliputian *Umwelt*. You'll never escape self-pity that way. What you ought to do is reach out, not draw in."

"I know I ought. Maybe. But I keep drawing in. I feel so stuffed I want to pass out . . ."

"Well, don't," says Lillian.

"I won't. How can I? I can't act on any one single thing because it's contradicted, with utmost truth, somewhere else. I've said to Sostana, 'Don't worry, an attractive woman like you, you'll marry again, a nice, responsible, loving man who'll love Mario and you. I hope you'll find somebody like Ezra or like my brother-in-law,' I say. I swear I'm not trying to make her jealous. I mean it, heart and soul. When I wish her that, I'm wishing her the kindest destiny I can think of. At that moment I believe in happy endings . . ."

"O the suffering," says Lillian, "the suffering in the world. People don't know how lucky they are to be well, to be with their families, until they hear about the suffering in the world . . ."

"What a disgusting idea!" says Hattie.

"But this disgusting idea," Ezra puts in, "that other people's afflictions make the dark border that sets off our own bright lives, seems to be what most people survive on. It's a nontruth that works for them . . ."

"It's like the contest of the sun and wind to make the traveler remove his coat. When the wind blows cold and threatening, we pull our coats tighter. We huddle."

"Wives with husbands in bed."

"Mothers with children at home."

"With families up the flights of stairs . . ."

"O the female attitude!" says Stanwood. "It makes a handle out of an idea, a bundle of bristles out of the varieties of human experience . . ."

"And uses the whole thing," Ezra says, "for a broom to sweep the hearth . . ."

"O I can hardly stand any more," says Hattie. "These television disasters. It doesn't matter that there's nothing new under the sun, and human types never change, and all this torture of man by man has happened before and before and before. Genghis Khan and the Inquisition and slave hunts. Not in our time! That's the difference. The terror of life and of human beings begins when you learn that all of it, all the brutality that's ever been in the world, has happened in your own time . . ."

"You mustn't watch," says Lillian.

"Listen!" says Ezra, "has it occurred to you—I mean this is supposed to be the great age of machine power—and look at what an extraordinary amount of plain old-fashioned fire-burning and ashes there's been! Look at Auschwitz. Even Hiroshima. What that really was was one fantastic fire."

"And? So? What's the meaning of all the burning?" Stanwood asks. "Is there a voice in the fire? Omens in the ashes?"

"Yes. Survival."

"Burn or fly up, is that it? Be ashes or phoenix!" Stanwood says. "Is that the message?"

"That is the message."

"You're sure that's the whole big-deal message."

"That is the entire up-to-and-including-this-moment message."

"Don't stand under no bombs, right?"

197

"That's it, brother."

"Brother-in-law."

"I mean."

"Just keep on running and clicking that camera, right?"

"You know what," says Hattie. "It would be something for a woman to try out, for once, that peculiar masculine despair that's so aggressive. Fuck everybody! The world is shit! Wonderful, soothing words. Like a lullaby. Get drunk for a whole night and in the morning come home and vomit on the rug. Somebody will clean it up, and it's a cinch that body will be female. Suppose as a woman, I said, 'The world is shit!' The next minute the baby cries and I rush to change its diaper and give it a drink of milk!"

"So that's out," says Stanwood.

"In fact, the more pregnant I get the more I feel myself sinking, like a stone, to the center of the earth. I want you, Ezra, to come straight home in the evenings . . ."

"I often do."

"And you mostly don't."

(I want you, Loftus, to stop this idiotic soul-searching with Erna. Come straight home.)

". . . And the more gravity-bound I become, the more lightfoot Ezra seems to feel. I swear his heels hardly touch the ground when he walks. You spring, like a man on the moon! I expect to see you take off from the fire escape one of these nights, airborne by Rolleis and Leicas."

"O what an idea . . ." Lillian sweeps crumbs from the cloth.

"You come in. My husband's vitality. Full of enthusiasm, pouches full of exposed film. Tumbling them onto the table. The little plastic-covered rolls of film—fuchsia, yellow, Kelly green. They cost a fortune. You like to shoot and shoot. He shoots like a millionaire. Like a maharajah on a hunt. Bang. Bang. Bang. You bang them all. The trophies on the kitchen table. And I'm muttering to myself, 'Why shoot so many? Why not select a few and shoot them? What's the big deal about a bagful?' "

(And you, Loftus, must you collect every last bit of evidence with Erna?)

"Honey, you know damn well why."

"I know. But my brain is muttering, 'What, again? What, so many? What, on the table, over the dishes, now—at dinnertime?' And I also know that the wifely thing, the intelligent thing, the only thing in which sanity or survival lies is to say, 'O wonderful!' Because you are home, and out there is the dark border."

The walls pause to breathe.

"It's Jean's turn. For God's sake, give Jean a chance. Say what *you* think . . ."

"Say what? Every side's expressed. Whoever distills you doesn't do you justice. . . ."

I am memorizing them for you, Loftus. I'll use them for a broom to sweep my hearth. . . .

Thirty |

Betrayal has come. I hold the letter in my hand. Not your letter. Whose letter, then? Hattie's. Whose betrayal? Listen.

". . . I saw it by accident, Jean. God help me, I must have been looking for it.

"Do you remember that creature who came in one evening when you were here? Yellow hair with a headache band, black eyes with blue-grease rims, the whites yellowish and bumpy, like mosaics, a tall girl with a bosom and a V-neck cashmere sweater and crutches, from a skiing accident? The one who was collecting signatures on a Ban the Bomb petition rolled up and stuck down the V? She's not on crutches any more. I wish she were. She's in and out of here all the time. Looking at Ezra's pictures—borrowing them to show to editors (she's supposed to be working for an editor of some kind)—then Ezra's supposed to go to her apartment and get them back. This time I went down and saw them together.

"My first thought was, Ezra really did mean to take her picture! Naked. Lying on the blue-green Scandinavian rug. Her skin powdery under the smoking lights. Ezra was dressed! That's what gave me hope for a minute. Dressed in his long-sleeved brown corduroy shirt I had *ironed* the day before. And he looked, *looked* as if he were about to shoot a picture. Head down, shoulders hunched, legs in a crouch, one desert boot between her knees, the other toed in beside her thigh. And then his hand on the bulb of her breast. It was an action picture. I had snapped it in mid-action at one one-hundredth of a second before I ran, developing in my mind, all the way back down the long corridor. . . . And Lillian trying to tell me he *was* only taking her picture. . . ."

I can hardly wait to finish this letter and start my own. At last, something to go on. An excuse for communication. My first real letter to you in a long time. Not just a note to say, so boringly and unconvincingly, Don't think of me, just work this out as best you can . . . but a letter, full of gossip and sex, something that will draw you close, Loftus.

"In Hattie's frenzy—imagine, darling—she bypassed the whole last weeks of her pregnancy and delivered herself of a fantasy infant son. (She and Ezra had already decided to name him Jacob, in honor of the martyrs of the TV trial, and I haven't had the heart to tell them it's a name despised by almost every New York Jew I've ever known, because of its corruptibility to Jake, as of Jake and Becky jokes.) This infant son she on the spot decided to kill, and kill herself, too, and scream while dying, so the whole house would hear and 'Ezra come running with his fly open and see us in our blood . . .'

"Then she changed her mind, only renounced him. 'Let him screw, we'll bolt, my son and I.'

"She imagined it was Christmas time. Balsam in the chapel, candlelight service, every pretty face aglow for God's party. All the pretty hymns, in four parts. Glee-club glee over mulled punch. She rocked her son. She sang, 'Phony, phony, phony, hurtiful and fright-y. . . .' But her parody faltered when she came to 'Early in the morning—' and sank altogether on 'my soul shall rise to thee.' She smiled while she sobbed, so her son should feel there was comfort in the world.

"But minutes counted. Already precious minutes wasted. To pull off the desert boots. The brown corduroy shirt, and fling it to crumple in a heap. The khaki pants. The boxer shorts, also freshly ironed.

"She screamed, No! at her son and he howled back, at his demon mother. She lifted him high as if to dash him to the ground, and out of the apartment again and running up two flights of steps to show her son 'Look! and always for your mother hate your father . . . !'

"And Ezra with gear and clothes on met her astonished in the hall. Saying, 'I just shot Hannah for the contest . . .' And Hattie screaming 'A-a-a-a-a-gh!' all down the brown hall. . . .

"But I can't send you this, my darling. One person's betrayal is too much like another's. . . .'"

Thirty-one |

Another piece of manuscript, the type blurred, smudged and struck over in many places, has detached itself, floated to the surface of the pile on my desk.

I've read somewhere that some people regard the child they were as a lost sister or brother. It must be the same with the child-woman you were when you fell in love with your husband. Who were you then? Another. A lost sister. How you envy her joy. How well you remember her pain. How angry you are she was deceived. How impatient with her stupidity. How you long to see her again. A lost, dear sister who died. . . .

Surely this one is Hattie's. It can't be my own. But in this day of the ubiquitous, portable Olivetti, who can say? No, it's Hattie's. Or else—my hands shake—I feel I've received, in some queer, wire-crossed way, a message from Erna. . . .

Thirty-two |

Late at night, the downstairs buzzer.

I buzz back and wait, the door to my apartment wide open, with a mixture of resignation and delight—like a parent who can look forward to visits only when the children's luck is bad.

But the young man who rounds the landing of the stairway—although he is wearing a black leatherette jacket identical with Jesús'—is someone I have never seen before.

It is too late for me to narrow my door.

"I am a buddy of Jesús," he says. Unlike Jesús, he is stocky, his feet seem to dig into the floor, and his arms stand away from his body like a wrestler's. His face is broad and flat.

"Where is Jesús?"

"He is in some trouble. I better come inside to tell you abou' that."

He sees me hesitate, sees exactly when I have decided I must risk it, and at that moment he walks in.

"What kind of trouble?"

"With the police." He is looking around with an air of

confirming everything he had expected to find. "He needs a lot of money. For protection, you know?"

"Does he?" I am growing angry and don't move from my spot in the entryway. In a minute I will throw him out. "I hope he gets it, then."

Jesús' buddy looks at me with feigned surprise. "You din' get me. You suppos' to give the money to me and I give it to him."

"If Jesús wants to speak to me, let him come. He doesn't have to send me a messenger."

Jesús' buddy turns his back on me abruptly and walks toward the bathroom.

"Let's see this famous hot shower you got."

I follow him. He has started to unbuckle his belt.

"I think I could use a hot shower."

"Listen!" I tap my hand on the arm of his jacket. "I suppose you must be a buddy of Jesús', or you wouldn't have known he came here. But I don't think he would send you. I think he would come himself if he could, or not send anybody. And if you don't leave now I'll call the police."

My head hits the edge of the toilet seat as I go down. Jesús' buddy goes down on top of me, ripping at my clothes.

I bang at him with my fists and I think, This ridiculous thing can't be happening to me.

My body is on the tile of the bathroom floor, my neck somehow bent between the two pedestals of toilet and sink. While I am trying to straighten it, he shoves his way in and begins to slam his hips against mine, pinching my nipples with his nails, smelling of sweat and garlicky hate.

What I am most conscious of is the cracking in my neck,

and after that the fact that the angle is all wrong, and he is prodding into the lower right quadrant where the sick ovary is taking a beating.

"Stop it, you're hurting! Just stop one minute so I can move! Please! Wait!"

The sound of my own voice uttering those time-worn futilities scares me more than this boy does. He answers with an exactness, as if someone had pasted the words up near his mouth, "Shut up! Don' give me that shit!"

His teeth grind, his nostrils dilate, his bad breath blows on me in steady gusts, his body is stupid and heavy beyond belief.

I try to move my hips in a round motion, to melt that rigid force, but he slams me back with his hips. Somehow I manage to straighten my neck, and to shift him to the center where, miraculously, nothing hurts. His body comes into sudden focus on my thighs and clitoris and I hear quite clearly Hattie saying, "Women's bodies can absorb anything." A sigh of relief escapes me. Almost at once he backs off, fixing me with a look of contempt for my body's accommodation, pulls up his pants and moves off, with a clumsy kind of trot, toward the living room.

I stand up at once and whisper into the water that quivers in the toilet bowl. "That wasn't so bad, it's over, I'm alive."

A spasm of nausea and dizziness knocks me down again and I vomit into the water and over the seat and the floor. When that's over I get up again and say to the water faucet, "That wasn't so bad. Now I'll wash my face with some cold water."

A premonition crawls along my backbone. I grab a towel to shield myself and run from the bathroom to see what he is doing. He has found my large, zippered manuscript bag beneath my desk. I shriek, "Don't touch my work!" and as he flings open the door, I yell after him, "Give it back!" He runs heavy-footed down the steps.

Two doors slam simultaneously. Mrs. Jensco's in the basement and the fag's with the silverfish upstairs. I creep to my bed.

A call from the police a little after 3:00 A.M. They have recovered my bag. Also Jesús' buddy, whom a clever-eyed young cop spotted racing along, carrying an expensive-looking initialed bag. A quick check turns up my name and address inside the bag. I am invited to the police station to claim my property, identify the thief and press charges. I stick to my refusal to do anything but the first of these things.

Jesús' buddy sits staring down at the wooden floor between his feet. Next to him stands a wizened little woman with a scarf over her head, crying into her hands. Her front teeth are missing, and someone has smashed flat the bridge of her small nose.

"I didn't really see him," I say. "I may have left the bag outside my door while I carried my grocery bundles in earlier in the evening. He may have passed it in the hall and thought someone was throwing it away. It is my bag, though, and I'm glad to have it back. And since I do have it back, I'm quite satisfied." I smile at the sergeant and at the clever-eyed young cop. "I'm grateful to you. I certainly would think you'd get a citation for this—it was quick work."

I discover that a button at the top of my hastily thrown-on dress is open. I button it. The sergeant looks on with interest. A new wave of nausea sweeps over me. I slump down into the chair next to Jesús' buddy.

The wizened woman moves forward on spindly legs.

"You don' know my boy!" she shrieks. "He is good! Only he got with some bad boys!" She points her finger ceilingward. "He sees my boy! He knows what I am sayin', that he is a good boy!"

"Shut up! She ain't pressin' charges!" the sergeant yells back.

I sign the papers and take my bag, like a found child, home.

Thirty-three |

Still the TV trial. Still the horrors coming with regularity, like something in nature—like rain, like cold. The machine guns punching bullet holes, the clubs beating against bone. The starving are starving, the screaming are screaming. Forever the bodies falling . . . the old Cinema 16 . . . *Meshes of the Afternoon* . . . the leaping figure is reversed, the leap sucked back. . . .

Hattie is lying on the couch, peering over her swollen belly, her eyes also swollen and red. I am on my chair.

Lillian bursts in. Her fairness mottled by a flush, her hand waving a letter. "Look! I took off early, I wasn't feeling well. When I got home I felt better, so I started straightening up some drawers. And now look, look what I found!"

She rouses Hattie, who seems almost asleep, drops the letter on Hattie's belly and the baby gives it a kick. It floats off like a leaf and then settles, quivering, next to Hattie on the sofa.

Lillian punches off the TV. "Read it!"

Then she sits on the sofa next to Hattie and starts to recite the sentences of the letter a beat or two ahead of Hattie, who is also reciting, so that we hear an imposition of words that would make no sense if we were not all three of us also reading:

My dearest wife Lillian, I am writing, writing this letter in case, in case, God forbid it, I should suddenly, suddenly against all my plans and will, will drop dead. I don't foresee what I foresee is I will live a long time, time and work like a horse every minute so that you, every minute, Lillian, will every minute have your desires which thank God are few and to see God are few my children if children are born God are few through college . . .

Lillian snatches the latter from Hattie and thrusts it at me. "For heaven's sake, you read it out loud, Jean."

I begin where I think we have left off.

". . . I frequently have myself in for a check-up, I am an absolute hypochondriac about it. So I have no worries about my health. And if our children, after they are born, are good enough students to warrant their having a college education, we are poor enough so that they will merit aid. Otherwise, if the other happens, if I drop dead before this is all carried out, you will see what has happened, that I have left you without a penny. But I don't for a minute believe this will happen. I truly believe that if I believed it would happen I could never have done what I have been doing over this period of time I am talking about. But. If I do drop dead. I understand, even with all the optimism I feel about my good health, that if it does happen and you, Lillian, and your sister, Hattie, are talking about it, and then later my children when they are old enough, that it might happen that you will think cynically about this and feel bitter. Then that's what I will think of, that will be my hell for eternity if I have any consciousness during the time when I am dying. If I drop dead. But most of the time, as I told you, I have good courage and good conviction that this will not happen. I have myself regularly checked and am in the best of health. It is only when I am overtired or rundown that I have nightmares about this. I don't as a rule allow myself to be tormented with this idea, because that would wear me down further and bring about the very thing I pray to God he'll spare us all.

You will understand everything from the boxes of letters in this drawer. There are almost five hundred letters. Almost five hundred children. If you read about them they will break your heart. And you will see the pictures. God forgive me, I could not resist those pictures. Sometimes I dreamed Ezra had taken those pictures. You can see why it was the Oriental children who haunted me most. Why do they say those faces are impassive? Those splayed toes. Those little torn pants and jackets sewn from sacks. Those wide faces, with so much room for sadness. Those sad, slanted eyes that should have been merry, like the eyes of the children playing on the bundles of sheets in the Chinese laundry, remember? Those little bowl-chopped caps of black hair. The heavy flower heads on skinny neck stalks. God, Lillian, forgive me!

"Our foursome, our snug square. You and I, Hattie and Ezra. I loved it. And the children to come would be in the center, like sweetest candy in the box. I had to break out somehow. I had to reach across a world to the children whose walls had all been torn away. It was the only way I could bear the richness of my castle.

"Lillian, every time I got my hands on money I sent it away to adopt a child. One hundred and eighty-five dollars gave a child food and clothing for a year. I sent away all our savings. The insurance premiums. Even the $25 account we started to get the bank's new depositor's gift. I bought you the electric clock at Bargainland for $5.95. Forgive me. Please don't be bitter. Never believe it was because I didn't love you. Look on it as my sickness. My excess that I couldn't hold back. Like Hattie's having to watch the trial. Like Ezra's infidelities. In everything else I was a moderate man. You sense so much without needing to be told. Pray with me for my long life . . ."

Hattie whispers, "Ezra's infidelities . . ."

Lillian sobs. "It's as if he'd already died. . . ."

The sisters send each other stricken looks. Reading the letter has made me a sister, too. . . . Here comes Stanwood's heart attack. . . . A gust of wind blows out the candle from that side of the room. . . . A wall of the house falls down. . . . A peg comes unstaked and a corner of the tent lifts up. . . . An animal meant to run on four legs now limps on three, scrawny, through the freezing city streets. . . .

"It's only a journal manuscript," I say, shivering with horror. "Words on paper."

"That's right, Lillian," says Hattie.

"Something people do to get themselves up in the morning, or to sleep at night . . . "

"That's right . . ."

"Like praying to the East . . ."

"Yes." Hattie touches finger tips to an overpowering yawn. She is sleepy most of the time now.

"Call up," Hattie says, struggling with her yawn, "Bargainland. . . ."

Lillian, crying, cannot remember the number.

Hattie gets Information, then at the store is told salesmen cannot receive personal calls. "It's an emergency!"

After a long wait Stanwood, breathless from dashing across the vast spaces of Bargainland . . .

"Stanwood! This is Hattie. What's this letter supposed to be, a farewell? We all love you. We need you . . ."

Hattie suddenly sobs. "Ezra's infidelities," she whispers into the phone. She listens at the receiver, pulls herself together, glances warningly toward Lillian. "No. Lillian did not find your letter. I did. I was looking in your apartment for . . . for . . ."

"In the shoebox," Lillian says in a low voice. She wipes her eyes.

". . . for some shoe polish. I'm sorry. It frightened me."

A pause. Hattie shakes her head at Lillian. "No. Lillian doesn't know. You didn't plan for it to be found, did you? Then we'll forget it. . . . What I think is that it's none of my business, I'm not supposed to have seen it. . . . Stanwood? Wait! I love you for it. . . ." She hung up.

"Do you?" Lillian, a trifle sullenly. "I'm not sure I do."

"Whatever it was, it wasn't selfish," Hattie says. "He wasn't thinking of himself."

"He wasn't thinking of me, either."

"What do you think, Jean?"

"I think the same as you, Hattie. That it's none of my business. I wasn't supposed to have seen it . . ."

"You should never tell him you know, Lilly."

"What? Let the little money we have trickle off into a bottomless bucket? Suppose I have a child?"

"Then he'd stop."

"And I'm to be penalized, insulted this way, if I don't?"

"Look at the man you married! Be glad. A man so tender-hearted, so vulnerable to little children's faces . . ."

"And lies right into his wife's . . ."

The sisters sit fuming on the couch.

"You defend Ezra to me," Hattie begins. "You condone what he does. To be led off by the nose by some pretty girls . . ."

"It's normal, at least. It's manly. It happens to men."

"And Stanwood . . ."

"No. That's womanly. To go to pieces over children. That's the woman in him. Now I wonder if that all has some bearing on why I don't have children . . ."

"It's nothing to do with man or woman," Hattie bursts out. "It's beauty of soul he's got. It's the feeling behind the action that matters. It's not selfish. I'd swap an Ezra for a Stanwood any day . . ." Hattie chokes over her own words and looks up, astonished.

Lillian is calm. "I'd swap, too. But Ezra," she adds primly, "is the father of your child. So it's out."

We all sit without speaking for a while. Then Hattie says soberly to her sister, "We've slipped out of our relationships. We'd better slip back in. . . ."

Thirty-four |

Hattie forgets, or else ignores, the fact that this time I was there, at the discovery of Stanwood's letter. She writes it all back to me again. But she adds something. Not everything is expressed within the four walls. Hattie reserves for me the erotic fantasy that follows Stanwood's letter.

"There's no end to my engorgement of other people's lives. Have you guessed, Jean, that I have even, in this same way, slept with my brother-in-law? But not—it's interesting—as my sister. No, as myself. In bed he was tenderness itself, and at the climax he burst into tears. O I was suddenly, horrifiedly conscious of my brother-in-law's large body in bed with me. I began to search around my darkened bedroom (I was supposed to be resting) hunting for a place to conceal the body. To be lying in the dark there! Sweating shamefully. To be harboring such doubleness— what? Triple! quadruple! in my own body. My heart trying to conceal its business from my son, his ear pressed to the wall of his womb room.

"Then comes Lillian, bending over me in the dark,

breathing anxiously and whispering, 'Are you all right? What is it, darling, any pain?' 'Go away, I'm not alone,' I pray. And the large white naked body very considerately gets up and passes through the wall.

"O Jean, I think of you! My free neighbor and friend. I think I can even see you behind your window, from my window. You are quitting work now, and gathering your pencils back into their jar, anchoring your designs with a paperweight. Or you are mixing yourself a drink, or getting ready to go out alone to have a very good dinner, then maybe to a movie alone, or coming back to read a book. Alone. Single. Independent. O solitude, dignified and austere. . . ."

I have already had so many *déjà vus* over Hattie's manuscripts that I tend to overlook them. But this phrase especially evokes an echo. I believe she may have written it to me before. Hattie repeats herself as she grows more literary. No doubt she, too, keeps a file cabinet—somewhat disordered—of notes that must be written up, and can't always remember which have already been done and which not.

But I can send you this—can't I, Loftus—without betraying anything or anybody?

Thirty-five |

"Dear Jean—

"We forgive them. Lillian is overlooking Stanwood's giving away money. I overlook whatever it is Ezra is giving away. Maybe he did shoot Hannah for the contest. Nothing is changed, but everything is changed. We've forgiven our husbands. What would be the use of not forgiving them? Everything is the same as it was. We are still a foursome. Nothing is the same. We never were a foursome. Only the wives believed that. Only women want life to be cosy, enclosed.

"I read somewhere, Jean, that some people regard the child they were as a lost sister or brother. It must be the same with the woman one was when one fell in love with one's husband. Who was I then? Another. A lost sister. . . ."

Hattie is repeating herself again. O Hattie, for God's sake, give birth! And then leave me alone. O solitude, dignified and austere . . .

Hattie also seems to have forgotten that I scan my *Times* every morning. When I come in to sit with her through the trial she gives me, these days, quick, tightlipped résumés of the day's news catastrophes.

It doesn't do any good when Lillian tells her, "Those are terrible things for a pregnant woman to be watching. Why don't you look at some of those serials they have? *As the World Turns* has serious things in it, too. . . ."

And it doesn't do any good when I tell her that I've read my paper. She has watched living clips on TV. She is in the news and the news is in her. There's no competing, news-wise, with a pregnant girl-woman whose membranes have all been alchemized to litmus paper. . . .

Thirty-six |

"My darling Jean—

"Your loving me must have revived or remade me. Erna sees something she didn't see before. You must have put it there. I was half-dead before I knew you. The last years of my marriage were dead. I was impotent with Erna. I have the feeling I wouldn't be any more. I have to be honest. I can't be anything less than honest with you. There is my promise to myself and to you. There is the pain for Erna. The pain for you, too, and for myself. But there are more years with Erna. Say that every year was a knife in the flesh. If Erna and I finish now for good, each of those knives will turn. Forgive me for burdening you with this. I love you. Don't stop loving me, I beg you. Bear with me. How much longer can this go on . . . ?"

Thirty-seven |

I no longer go to watch the trial with Hattie. One day when she called at her usual hour with her usual question I took up, for the first time, the option her question had always implied.

"I'm just swamped with work, Hattie. I'll have to skip it for a while."

"Oh!" she said. Then, "Shall I check with you tomorrow?"

"Well, what I think now is that it's going to take a while. Let me call you when things ease up."

For a long minute her silence filled my ear. Then she blurted, with an incomparable mixture of innocence and disbelief, "But the whole thing won't last much longer, Jean!"

I knew what she was including in that "whole thing." Her pregnancy, her extrasensory perception or whatever it was—her belief, at least, in her ability to slip inside the lives of other people—that, plus one other idea that hung from our telephone connection and made the instrument so heavy in my hand that I felt I had to prop both elbows on my desk and lean my forehead into my other hand. And that idea was that I was abandoning them—that special group whose agonies we had somehow, by our attention, held in the circle of our arms: the far-gone pregnant women in their forced march; the woman giving birth in the typhus-lice-infested straw; the woman who was shot but did not die, and who dug her way from under a mountain of corpses that spouted blood; those gaunt ascetics of the camps, the Muslims, who had passed beyond hunger and terror, and the children, who had not. . . .

Now Hattie would hold them in her arms alone.

Thirty-eight |

Lillian calls me.

"I don't know how you stood it for so long, Jean. You were marvelous to come and watch with Hattie as long as you did. I made her solemnly promise not to turn the thing on any more when she's by herself. I wish I could take off from work these last couple of weeks to be with her, but I just can't. I've gotten a full-time secretarial job. No more temporary things, and Ezra takes all his own stuff around now. You know our financial situation. It's too bad, but that's the way it is. May I ask one more favor? She can hardly walk, she waddles so, but she's gotten it into her head to go to the Metropolitan Museum tomorrow afternoon. It seems to be terribly important to her, and none of us can talk her out of it. Maybe she thinks she'll make an artist out of her child—God knows what she's gotten into her head. But she really shouldn't go alone. I thought Ezra might, but no, he's got an appointment to photograph the interior of some church or other, and Stanwood doesn't dare miss a day. Could you possibly find the time, Jean? I hate to ask. I know how busy you are. . . ."

✧   ✧   ✧

Hattie walks, her coat on and bursting open between the buttons, among the bare-breasted women in the Museum's sculpture hall.

"I want to see the mothers," she says. So we walk. I am thin and fidgety, flattened down by all this beating against the stream. She is enormous. She rolls down the corridors. The two of us are a far cry from the classical norm of these near-naked female forms.

The little stone children have hair that lies like snakes on their shoulders, garments melting along their thighs. They cling and stumble and clasp at the ankles and buttocks of their marble mothers who stride, unbelievably serene, on broken toes, with hands severed at the wrists.

"Mothers, holy mothers," Hattie whispers to the lopped women.

My presence, when she recollects it, brings on an afterthought of embarrassed irony. "I don't know *why* I felt I had to see them."

She reaches around herself with effort and presses her hands against her back. She has become sway-backed in spite of the exercises, which I know a great deal about. She has sent me, scattered through her letters, a complete instruction manual (if I should ever take the trouble to piece it together) of natural-childbirth exercises.

". . . You lie back on the mat, the knees drawn up in a practice bearing-down. . . .

". . . You lie back on the mat, you concentrate on opening everything . . . don't tighten . . . open completely. . . .

". . . You lie back on the mat . . . you inhale deeply through the nose . . . exhale in a series of short, shallow pants . . . practice working up to a full minute. . . ."

Hattie opens her hands and stares in at the redness of her palms. Then she turns her hands over again and glances nervously at her watch.

"How do you feel?" Some instinct nudges me.

"All right, I guess. A little strange. But I always feel a little strange now."

She is silent for a moment. Then suddenly she digs into her pocket and takes out a newspaper clipping.

"This was in the *Tribune*. They must not have had time for it in the televised part of the trial. This is what one of the witnesses said."

Her hand and her voice are both shaking. "Please, may I read it to you?" Her whisper echoes among the marbles. " 'The children were covered with sores. They had diarrhea. They screamed and wept all night in the empty rooms where they had been put. There was nothing in the rooms but filthy mats full of vermin. Before dawn, our women crept among the children, trying to comfort and clean them. But there were no clean cloths, the water was icy cold. Terror had overcome them. The halls were a madhouse. When the orders were given to take the children to Auschwitz, it was as if they sensed what was in store. Then the police would go up and the children, screaming with terror, would be carried kicking and struggling to the courtyard. . . . '"

Carefully and slowly, Hattie folds the clipping again and returns it to her pocket without looking at me.

I feel something like a great scream rising in this silent sculpture hall. These goddesses stand, arrested in movement, as if just now their limbs had been shattered, just now their eyes struck blind, just now their bodies turned to stone

Hattie and I start walking toward the whale's belly of the Museum lobby.

"Do you know something I've been thinking?" Hattie says, after a while.

I ask myself if there can be anything I don't know. . .

"I want to write a play—" she stutters with embarrassment—"I've never written a thing in my life. . . ."

I think of the pounds of manuscript on my desk, and in all the drawers. "Well, why not?"

"Because I had a sort of a vision." She glances sidelong at me. I keep my face half-turned away, glancing at paintings. I don't want to force her to reach for the ironic afterthought ("I don't know *why* I had to have a *vision*.") "All the mothers . . . all those tormented children, Jean. We saved them with our bodies. The babies in the lice straw. The ones who cried alone all night . . . the others . . . all of them . . ." She peeps at me again, afraid to speak, almost . . . then, "We drew them into our wombs and kept them safe till danger was past . . . you know? Then, easily, gently, we passed them out again in a warm coating of blood. . . ."

I am pretending to memorize a Botticelli. But Hattie's vision leaps into me and warms some old, long-frozen grief.

"Do you think it's crazy?" she whispers.

"No," I whisper back. If one of us is going to weep, let it not be me.

"You're sure? It's not silly—not ridiculous?"

"No, it's not." I look at her fully now. Her face looks older, prepared for suffering. "It would have been wonderful. If women could really have done that. Take back as lovingly as they gave . . ."

"Thank you, Jean. I couldn't have told anyone but you."

She lets out a pent-up breath and seems to shake herself free of her own awe. "As a vision it was so convincing. Afterward I worried whether it might seem like—you know—a vacuum cleaner. But now, what to do with it?" She flushes with embarrassment. "You can't write up a vision. It's got to be a play, or a story, or something people can understand. . . ."

"Well—why not?"

"It must be the baby coming . . . I'm not really creative. . . ."

She doesn't yet know the exact working out of the play, if it's really a play. But she feels its rhythms. In her mind she sees the lighted stage and she feels, like a choreographer, the rhythms of her characters (as yet unknown) as they move through their lives. She says she feels it also like a song without words.

"I can almost sing it to myself," she says. "Do you know what I mean?"

Her eyes, like everything else about her, seem to be brimming over. Her coat is bursting open, her swollen feet shuffle along in Ezra's loafers. She seems to have shrunk in height a foot or so. If I put a hand on her she would topple and crack open like Humpty Dumpty.

I feel a curious tightening at the bottom of my belly.

"Let's take a cab to my apartment and have a cup of coffee," I say.

Hattie checks her watch. "It's a little after four. Let's go to mine."

She seems half-asleep on her feet as I wave from the curb for a taxi.

Thirty-nine |

We start to drink our coffee. Then, like an addicted child, Hattie turns on television.

"O let's not," I say, as casually as I can.

"I don't watch alone," she pleads. "But now that you're here . . ."

It all begins again. The music. The dragging sound. The masked faces. The disembodied voices. The clubs, the bullets, the bodies, the nothingness. . . .

A torrent is flushing from under Hattie's skirt. Down her legs and onto the wooden floor. It's as if she has finally come up with an appropriate response to what she has been watching for so long. Her whole body weeps, gushes forth a torrent of tears. Hattie stands up. She looks down at herself. More torrents. Her skirt is drenched. Ezra's loafers fill up.

"I suppose that must be it," Hattie murmurs in a dazed voice. "That's the bag of waters. It broke."

I feel sick. I am getting menstrual cramps. Where the hell is her *family*, that famous foursome? I am no relative.

"Where's your doctor's number? I'll call him and you get

your bag. Don't be frightened," I say, my heart hammering. "We'll get a taxi."

She gives me a funny look. "But my labor hasn't started yet."

She is torn between the television set and the warning of the drenched floor.

I punch the set button off. "Are you crazy?" I say furiously. "You've got to get going! I'll leave a note for Ezra." I am beginning to run around her kitchen, looking for a pencil and a piece of paper, forgetting that I carry these things in my purse.

Lillian is suddenly here. She has used her key and apologizes when she sees us standing there. "I thought you might be napping, Hattie. I got so restless at work—I don't know what got into me—I just told them I felt sick and I had to leave early." Then she sees Hattie's drenched skirt and the spreading pool.

When the sisters are finally ready, Lillian's cheeks are flushed scarlet, Hattie's are pale limes. We have a quick, paranoid conference about cab fare, and empty all purses for change in case the cab driver refuses to take them because he cannot change a bill, or shows some other fanatical barrier to sanity.

When they finally go out I stay on to write a note to Ezra and to clean up. I use paper towels to soak up the amniotic fluid. It is as clear and odorless as water. I feel I ought to save it in a vial, like Jordan water. The waters of Jordan flow over my hands.

I am exhausted, nearly tottering, when I get back to my apartment. It is seven o'clock. I haven't dared for weeks to call you. Now I tell myself you'd want to know about Hattie.

For some reason I am stunned to find you there in your apartment when the phone rings.

"Loftus—listen!—I haven't called for any other reason than to tell you—not to pressure you or to reproach you or anything, only to tell you—I just finished wiping Hattie's birth fluid off the floor. She's having her baby."

"Did you really do that, Jean? My God, what did I get you into!"

"I feel I want to pray for her."

"Do it then." Loftus' voice is distracted. Who is standing beside him?

"Who am I supposed to pray to? Is that all you have to say? Aren't you going to tell me anything that's happening—just this silence?" I've caught an image of a large, glossy desk with the name in blocky type: MARRIAGE COUNSELOR. Erna sits at one side, Loftus at the other. Behind the desk sits an intelligent tape recorder.

"I'll tell you what Hattie tells me. Sometimes I think I invented you out of my need! Do you exist?"

I am shouting it into the tape recorder. Somehow my point of the triangle has got to be wedged in, too.

The anguish in your voice appalls me. "I can't talk piecemeal, Jean. I *will* write. It's all in my mind. I only have to get it down. I have such a strong feeling that all this is coming to a right conclusion for us now. But I don't want to do anything that . . . Jean, do you remember the Rube Goldberg cartoon you wrote me about? Jean?"

"I didn't think I wrote that to you. I thought I only thought about that . . ."

"It was very apt. The children are in this now. I don't want any of us to jostle the wrong lever and have something, far down the line, jump out at us later. I want to do this right. Jean? Please. Please!"

"Of course. I really only called to tell you Hattie's having her baby."

"Bless them both. Bless you."

". . . And you. . . ."

Forty |

In the middle of the night, Lillian phones from the hospital. She is crying in the waiting-room phone booth.

"A dry birth. A long labor. Hard. Pray for her. . . ."

I have been lying down—between phone calls—with your robe on. I told myself, I am putting this on the way primitives put on the skin of the animal whose powers they need to acquire in order to be a match for him. I stored that up as something to amuse you with later—farther down the line—where there would be no jostling. But then all I did was to cry all over the robe, spoiling the foulard.

I lie down again, overcome once more with menstrual cramps. A knotting of the lower belly. Dry. Hard.

The downstairs buzzer scares me from a doze. I sit up and stare into the darkness, trying to picture whose hand on the buzzer. Jesús' buddy. Back (since I have not pressed charges) for more. One of the foursome. Someone dragging himself up to tell me in person that Hattie's labor has been lost.

I wait to hear if the buzzer will sound again. It doesn't.

I walk with the slowness of my own executioner to the buzzer and then crouch behind my barely open door peering into the hallway like some dotty old recluse trying to stave off the bad news from outside.

But no, the steps are light and bounding . . .

"I been keepin' away. Okay if I come in now?"

As soon as the door is closed behind us I glare at him.

"Listen, Jesús, did you send somebody to me for money?"

"No, I din' sen' nobody. Did somebody come?"

My fury of mixed emotions has suddenly collapsed. I hesitate.

"Wouldn't you want them to?"

"To come up here? No. I don' think so."

"Why wouldn't you want them to come?"

He looks puzzled and then he says softly, "It's my own place that I foun' myself. If any of my buddies came, I don' think it would be so special for me no more."

"Nobody came. I just wondered why you hadn't tried to get in touch with me."

"Here I am. I came to get in touch with you my own self."

"All right. I'm glad you came. Now you can help me, Jesús. A friend of mine is in the hospital having a baby. You're Catholic, aren't you? How would you pray for a woman who's having a baby?"

He takes me in with a glance—all of it, the lumpy robe, the red eyes, the matted hair—and sighs, like a priest who sees an outlying parishioner going downhill. He himself is thinner, altered. He seems to be rounding some bend away from his young manhood.

Still in his black simulated-leather jacket, he kneels and clasps his hands and bows his head.

"Dear Mother of God," he begins—his bony chest lifts with another sigh—"look after my frien' who is sufferin' in the hospital, and . . . uh . . . take care of her . . . an' . . . uh . . . give her a easy delivery . . . for the sake of the Son you bore. . . ."

He drops his arms to his sides, but keeps his head down a moment longer, tilted a little to the right, as if listening now to the response. His face is thinner than last time. His cheeks hollower, his lips fuller. His eyelids shine and quiver over his closed eyes.

"Thank you, Jesús. That's nicer than mine would have been. . ."

He opens startled eyes and gets to his feet. "Well . . . somethin' like that . . ."

"Would you like to hear mine?"

He shrugs. "Okay."

"Dear God—" Jesús fiddles with his jacket zipper, which is now fixed, I see—"God of the medical-experiment cell block . . . God of the common lime-pit grave . . . God of chopped fingers . . . of blinded eyes, God of electrodes attached at one end to a jeep battery and at the other to the genitals of political prisoners, God, most powerful God of all these things . . ."

Jesús steps backward. "What are you talkin' about . . . you crazy?" He begins to rezip his jacket.

"Violence. I thought you would understand about violence . . ."

"You don't pray to the Holy Virgin like that!" He heads for the door.

"Wait! I'm sorry if I offended you. Don't go. I was going to end my prayer the same as you did. . . ."

His face is stubbornly outraged.

"I was, Jesús. I was going to say, 'God of all these things, give Hattie an easy delivery.' "

Jesús looks down at his jacket. "Why I came, I could use a hot shower. . . ."

Through the window, under lamplight, I see his buddies lounging in the street, smoking.

While Jesús is showering, while his buddies are lounging and looking up at my windows, while you, Loftus, are inching along the delicate mobile of your relationships, while Hattie is laboring and God is filing prayers, the phone rings again. It is Stanwood, his voice breaking.

"Hattie has given birth to a daughter. They're both fine."

"Thank God!"

"Amen!" Stanwood says.

Forty-one |

What am I doing in the street, hailing a taxi in midmorning?

I am going to the hospital to see the new baby, to visit Hattie, to observe firsthand the wonders of modern hospitalization that make possible the most advanced care of every patient.

There are four beds, with four women in them, in each of the rooms on the maternity floor. The beds are close, they have curtains between them through which every sound passes. It is like one of those dreadful apartments in a Dostoevsky novel, where all suffering and joy take place behind thin partitions.

I wait in the doorway, because Hattie is talking to her obstetrician. Her curtain is partly drawn, but their conversation resounds through the room. Hattie is imploring her doctor to tell what it was she said while drugged.

"I know I said things. I have snatches of words stuck to my brain . . ."

Dr. Folsom has a matchstick stuck to the fibers of his raw silk tie. "What do women say? Everything. Anything. Some say, 'Stop the magazines.' Some say, 'Chop the liver.' What do you care? And stop berating yourself because the natural childbirth didn't work out. You have your baby. Why do you have to know what you said?"

"There was all that pain. There must have been some moment of truth . . . I want to know what really goes on in my head . . ."

"If you must know, you were concerned about making a bowel movement on the table."

"Oh!"

"Listen. Take your pills. Sit on your rubber tube. Enjoy your baby. And—ah! that's nice, you have a visitor."

He flees behind another curtain.

"I love that man," Hattie says to me. "I love him. His hands were on my belly the whole time."

I have already read part of her postlabor special, which she dispatched at once to me, via Ezra.

"I thought he didn't show up till the end. I thought you said they left you all alone?"

"Did I? Well, you know what? I can't really remember any more. . . ."

She grasps my hand. Her hand feels hot and full of life.

"Jean! I'm so glad you came! I just nursed the baby. Then they took them away for naps. What a shame you missed her. You can go to the nursery later and look through the window. A beautiful, beautiful girl. When the baby cries—they say you can tell your own—you feel your milk come down like solid blocks. . . . I feel so happy . . . suddenly overcome . . . in spite of everything, you know . . . ?"

Hattie's hair is pulled back with a pink ribbon. Lillian

must have been at her hair. Her forehead gleams with a greenish shine, enormous black rings beneath her eyes.

"I have my play!" she whispers, and beckons me closer, her green forehead shining up at me from her pillow. "Listen, Jean! It's to be set in a hospital room—like this—with four mothers. The spirits of children fly above them in the air—like angels, you know?"

She stops to consider. "They'll have to be suspended on wires or some kind of pulley thing," she adds practically.

"The mothers talk about their love for their children— it's different for each one, you know, what it means, the words they find—and then the children talk about their happiness to be alive at first, and then each tells how he or she died. After each war, each atrocity, each death, the children fly down to their mothers' beds and disappear in them. Then the whole thing is repeated, and the children fly up again. New children . . . new births . . . new times . . . new joys. . . . Centuries and centuries and centuries of joyful births and terrible deaths. . . . After a while we begin to see similarities . . . we see the same children over and over . . . those children haven't been lost . . . !"

Once again my body experiences the sensation of being filled by Hattie's visions. For a second a clamp—one that I hadn't even been conscious was there—seems to unlock from my lungs at the thought that *those children haven't been lost*. At the same time, when those children's spirits fly down to their mother's beds, I know what it is that's suctioning them in. Hattie has not given up on her female vacuum-cleaner idea. All I have to do is flip a mental switch, and Hattie's Great Suctioning Ingatherer is turned off.

237

The image is bizarre, but Hattie's joy that at last she has won her vaginal shell game with the *Einsatzgruppen*—six million cats in a hat—outshines it.

"Ezra will do big photo blow-ups for scenery—concentration camps, death cells, nooses, knives, racks, operating rooms—nothing will be too old-fashioned or too modern. . . . You'll design the programs . . . Stanwood will find all the bed props . . . Lillian will go out and get backers. . . ." Her face shines with yellow-tinged excitement.

"Does God see us, Jean?"

I shrug in a way that allows, I hope, for doubt, the way you do with a child who can't for the moment cope with another "no."

"You don't think so?"

"It seems irrelevant, that's all. Isn't it enough that we see each other? Witnessing and being witnessed without end?"

Her eyes water above the blue bruises. The pink ribbon sits askew on her head like a hastily pinned-on medal—an afterthought for a frightened soldier who got caught in the bombardment.

No one has come in response to repeated rings on Hattie's buzzer, so I go out into the hall and steal a *papier-maché* vase from an unlocked supply closet. I arrange the flowers I've brought and set them on the crowded little table next to Hattie's bed. Then I help her limp to the bathroom, wait for her, and then help her limp back again to bed. I kiss her good-by and run off to see her daughter. But the nursery curtains have already been drawn.

Forty-two |

Back on my street—street of rubble and sudden disappearances—I look up, as Hattie said you used to do, Loftus. By the scatterings of brick-and-stone dust, or by a trick of sunlight—it is very faint, a suggestion only—my window looks X'd out.

I pound up the steps. I am ready to yell, "Don't touch my work!" to the wreckers. I expect to see them tossing my belongings into a heap, the door broken through, the shelves ripped from the walls.

But on the landing of the first flight I stop. Suppose there are no wreckers? No chaos, no flying belongings and splintered wood? Suppose there is only an empty room? Suppose, behind the painted X, nothing at all?

The hall, in fact, is utterly quiet. My door is locked shut. My keys are where they always are in my purse—although for a minute I thought they weren't; I couldn't locate them with my finger tips—and they open the door. I see, first thing at the far end of the room, my disordered desk.

I rent an apartment, *donc j'existe.* . . .

239

On my desk is Hattie's half-read, postlabor special—a fat manuscript, the pregnancy puffiness still not yet gone down. . . . I sit before it, grateful to find it there, ready to sink into it, the dear dull details, so boringly believed in and *there* (Hattie sends me manuscripts, *donc j'existe*).

But how is it possible? Did I really fling your letter on the table as if it were ordinary mail and not see it, not feel that it was there, even though covered by Hattie's big envelope? But it is there, a prize, a present. More precious, because unexpected. Joy leaps up; then joy leaps down. I reach, then unreach for the letter.

It's possible my not knowing made better sense. I may have seen, then unseen the letter, then flung it just this way, a potential landmine over which a body—Hattie's manuscript—threw itself in the nick of time. Haven't I just experienced a near-coronary, pounding up half the steps, then creeping up the remainder to see whether my apartment existed? I am not ready to go through that so soon again.

I put off reading some of my letters, *donc j'existe* a little longer.

A manuscript? A book? A play?

A postlabor special.

. . . *At first everything was pleasant, joking. Then everybody disappeared. The pretty little student nurses went off duty, taking their unicorn heartbeat listeners, their clipboard charts. . . . We were two in the Labor Room. The pains began to come hard to the woman in the next bed, a Spanish woman. Even the tall, skinny Indian intern and the short, curly-haired Italian one stopped coming around to "dig for potatoes." That's what the Spanish*

*woman called it when they put their fingers in, to see how
much she was dilated.*

*"Mother of God, what are you digging for, potatoes?"
She moaned a lot. Then everybody disappeared. Finally
the Spanish woman began to yell a lot. . . .*

The letter, the manuscript, is written in a nervous,
scrawling hand, dashing over pages. Hattie's manuscript
mania combined now with the new mother's mania to talk
out the shock of birth. She must have packed reams of
paper in her hospital bag, along with the new nightgown
and slippers and beribboned robe that Lillian had given
her. . . .

Now I know what happened to Hattie when she spoke of
"sideslipping" into another's experience. Now, with your
unopened letter waiting there—I am determined not to
touch it yet, determined to stick it through with Hattie
first—I slip in, I see the whole thing, I am in the Labor
Room with the Spanish woman (she is Jesús' mother, having the stepfather's baby). Hattie's manuscript guides me
like a scenario. She has written a play, and I am in it.

*Indian Intern (skinny back curving inside white jacket,
dark wrists and big bony hands hanging from too-short
white sleeves): Excuse me. I must now examine you.*

Spanish Woman: Mother of God.

*(Indian Intern draws curtain halfway between two
beds. Crouches at foot of Spanish Woman's bed and
stretches long arm toward twin hills of her legs.)*

*Spanish Woman: Mother of God! what are you digging
for?*

(Indian Intern does not reply, continues scooping,

241

squeezing. After a while Indian Intern departs, leaving curtain still partly drawn.)

Spanish Woman: Mother of God, how that hurt! I wonder do they really have to do that, or what?

Hattie: I wish I could help you.

Spanish Woman: Don't you have your pains?

Hattie: Not so much yet. You're ahead of me. My turn will come and you'll be all finished. You'll feel fine.

Spanish Woman: You don't have to sound so ashamed of it. Sure your turn will come. This time I'd like to skip my turn.

(Indian Intern comes back with second Intern. Short, Italian, with curly dark-blond hair and tan face.)

Spanish Woman: Listen, it hurts a lot. Can't you please give me something?

(Indian Intern steps back politely to allow Italian Intern to approach Spanish Woman's bed. Italian Intern stretches forth stocky arms and probes and squeezes. Spanish Woman moans. Italian Intern turns face past right shoulder to speak to Indian Intern.)

Spanish Woman: Get out of there! Get out of there!

(Italian Intern ignores her and goes on as before, probing and talking to Indian Intern.)

Spanish Woman (whimpering): Help me. Help me, God!

(Italian Intern withdraws hand and removes rubber glove, wrist to finger, snap! Opens clip on his clipboard and lets it shut, snap! Removes ballpoint pen from pocket of white jacket and presses thumb to button, click! Writes as he and Indian Intern move toward door. Has not once spoken to Spanish Woman or looked at her face.)

Spanish Woman: Help me! Give me something.

242

(*Both interns move toward door.*)

Spanish Woman: (*Her voice goes deep as a man's and so strong it fills the room and seems to shake all the curtains*): *I'm talking to you!*

Indian Intern (*turns and speaks from remote height*): *Later.*

Spanish Woman: It hurts me now!

Indian Intern: Your physician has not called to indicate medication.

Spanish Woman: Listen, I don't even know his name. He was somebody at the clinic.

Indian Intern: No doubt he will call at a certain time.

Spanish Woman (*her voice turns womanly again as she speaks reasonably, sweetening her tone, cajoling from the bed*): *If he was here he would see I'm suffering and give me something. If you won't call him then you give me something. That makes sense, don't it?* (*Now whispering in sweet, trembling voice.*) *God will bless you for it.*

(*Indian Intern turns, unbribed, to go. Italian Intern leaves, scribbling.*)

Spanish Woman (*voice blasting out again*): *God curse you!* (*Whispering again*) *God help me help me help me.*

Indian Intern (*turns again and looks at Spanish Woman with surprise*): *Have you never been told that a woman brings forth her child in pain? This is the punishment of God in your own religion, is it not?*

Spanish Woman: O God help me. God help me!

Indian Intern (*glancing at Hattie*): *Do as this woman. Keep silence.*

Hattie (*protesting*): *But I don't have pain.*

Indian Intern (*sternly*): *Then you will have no child.* (*He leaves.*)

Spanish Woman (*slow crescendo and three short bursts, like dolorous cheers, from behind curtain*): *Ayee, ay! ay! ay!*

Hattie (*calling over*): *Don't worry, they'll come now. They heard you. They'll come running from all directions.* (*Looks toward doorway, which remains empty. Cries repeated, louder, behind the curtain.*)

Hattie (*rolls onto her side, lets feet dangle down to footstool and slowly sits up. Rubs hands over lower part of belly, as if just beginning to feel ache there. Steps onto bare floor and walks, half-crouching, over to other bed. Peers around curtain*): *O, O your face! As if it's being squeezed in a vise!* (*Looks down the woman's body.*) *Dear God, there's blood. Clots of blood and mucus. Look, below, where it's shaved—they shaved me too—it's oozing like a wound. . . .* (*Hattie's hand reaches out as if to smooth the face, but draws back, afraid. She whispers*): *I'll get help.*

(*Hattie makes slow way out to corridor. Half-crouched, fingers locked under belly, weight seeming to hang between her legs. Corridor is deserted.*)

Hattie: No one told me this is how it would feel. My whole belly clenched into a fist, and clenching tighter than I ever imagined it could, before it gives way.

(*Crouches convulsively and lands on hands and knees. Lets out piercing scream.*) *O God don't let my baby fall out and smash on this floor.*

Spanish Woman: Jesus! Lemme die!

(*Hattie is crouched on cold Kemtile. The long corridor deserted. Toward the end of the corridor, a wooden desk, with no one at it, beyond that a window, a glaring rectangle. Behind Hattie, suddenly, a voice.*)

Voice: What the hell are you doing out here!

Hattie (turns head to look up. Sees starched Head Labor Nurse, gigantic in indignation. Hattie, from dog's position, directs): Help that woman!

Head Labor Nurse (Lights from rectangle glare in eyes): Don't tell me what to do. You just get back in there!

I am in no mood for this dialogue. Not while that blue envelope is burning a hole in my corner vision. Grab seven or eight pages of this scrawl and shove them under the pile.

Now we are in the Delivery Room. Klieg lights glare down on the table. Ah, the obstetrician at last, handsome in his white coat.

"Son of a bitch, where have you been till now?"

But Hattie's mangled tongue might have uttered instead some grateful endearment, such a pleased smile, she says, he bestowed on what he saw between her legs.

Now the paper itself is different. Gray, pulpy, lined. A questionnaire, in fact.

The hospital administration would appreciate your comments on any aspect of your stay here, so that we may continue to do everything to ensure the comfort and well-being of our patients. How did you find the hospital food? Was your room comfortable? How was the nursing staff? (Rate Excellent, Good, Fair.) Did someone answer promptly when you rang the buzzer in your room?

Hattie had scratched a thick, angry stroke through all that and had written:

✓ ✓ ✓

245

*When I was in the Labor Room it was like being in a con-
centration camp. And I am not the only woman (she had
crossed out* woman *and wrote, no doubt with pride,*
mother) *who says so. All the mothers I talk to here say
they were treated like prisoners. The interns have no feelings. They listen to the screaming and it doesn't affect
them. You ask them: How many fingers am I dilated, so
you'll know how many times per minute to pant, and they
look right through you. One of the nurses said I could never
nurse a baby with such small nipples. She tried to discourage me and undermine my confidence. My nipples may be
small, but they're all right with my baby. She likes to take
milk from my breast far more than she does from a bottle,
no matter how big the nipple is. The nursery head nurse
told me they have trouble getting my baby to take milk
from the bottle at the two o'clock feeding. So it seems my
baby would prefer to drink from my breast at two in the
morning, but I need my sleep because I am so tired from all
I have gone through these last few days including the sa-
distic indifference to pain of the SS guards in the X-ray
room. And also (she had turned over the sheet of pulpy
paper, ignoring the ink that showed through, and wrote
sprawlingly on the reverse side) all the women here say the
same thing although they do not wish to sign the petition
I made up because I understand now they are grateful also
superstitious about their new babies and the hand that
rocks the cradle doesn't care to rock the boat it seems. I
can sympathize because I don't want any of what I am
now writing to touch my child. I am beginning to see how
it is with women and I see that if I were going to do anything about gathering them together I should have done
it long ago when I would not have seen I was bound to*

246

fail. But now I know too much and haven't even the strength to try and circulate any more petitions and to fail to get them filled. And also I would have had to do it before my baby was born which is a time when everything gets mixed up for a while inside a woman's head even if she was able to keep it more or less straight before. All the little tiny details mixed with the big things (you can see why—babies thrive on all the tiny details.)

I have a beautiful daughter who seems to take a happy view of life for which thank God, and I will do nothing to discourage this because anything she is capable of attempting she must attempt before she knows the truth and that is best. Everyone in the nursery has been most helpful and is to be thanked for the good health of my baby, except for the nurse who said my nipples were too small (she is a Negro, which is the saddest part).

I can tell you that if the women in this maternity ward weren't (a) exhausted and (b) delirious over their babies and (c) so superstitious, which I am sure must be traceable to something much more serious than superstition, some very high ideal for themselves and a great discipline of their actions to motherhood, they would not only sign petitions but would make such an outcry that you would have a mutiny within these walls and nothing at this hospital would ever be the same again!

The gray pulp gives way to Hattie's usual white manuscript paper.

We are back in the room with the four beds, setting for Hattie's play within (without?) a play. Groans and sighs from the new mothers. Stitches stick, wounds burn. Defecation is bloody agony. The bladder, battered senseless, cannot yet bring itself to wring out even one drop of urine. The threat of the catheter, with its burning tip, hangs over the room.

"It's true, you do forget a lot."
"They're all understaffed. They haven't got time to treat you like a human being."
"When I had to have an X ray, there was this marble slab and I had to creep naked over, not even a sheet over the hard coldness of it . . ."
"They haven't got time to treat you like a . . ."
"They hear screaming and see blood all day. They get hardened. Otherwise they'd . . ."
"Just the same, I thought to myself, this could be what hell is like . . ."

There was talk of a protest until the babies were brought, in their white blankets, to nuzzle and suck and bestow their hypnotic peace.

Hattie listless in bed. The nurse's aide presents a rectal thermometer to her mouth. She shakes her head, no (the nurse's aide: Listen, are you gonna co-operate or not!), then gives in. It tastes darkly bitter and she chokes down an impulse to gag, reasoning that it is only the disinfectant. Afterward, she says to Mrs. Volpe in the next bed, *"I just had to put a rectal thermometer in my mouth."* Mrs. Volpe makes a face. *"Tell the head nurse, otherwise they'll just keep doing it. They have no decent help in these hospitals. I went to the bathroom before and there was no paper. Can you imagine? In a hospital!"*

Half-whispering, half-asleep: *"Shall we make up a peti-*

tion, Mrs. Volpe?" "Shhh. Rest. Just tell the head nurse, dear. Good night."

A volunteer in a lavender apron sits on Hattie's bed. *"I've brought some magazines. We're having a bit of post-partum depression, aren't we, dear?"*

"No. I'm like this."

Forty-three |

I have come, by scanning and skipping, to the end of the sequence. But some loyalty to Hattie's dilemmas (or maybe it's simply that I'm not yet ready to know what's in your letter) sends me back to pick up Hattie where she still crouches on all fours in the corridor. Time, under the glittering eye of the Head Labor Nurse, has been suspended. Hattie still crouches, still gasps out her part of the dialogue:

"Help that woman!"

"Don't you dare give me orders!"

The fist squeezes itself again. And when she thinks she's in perfect balance with it—her held breath and its clenched force—it tightens its grip in a convulsion of tightness. And Hattie has no inhale or exhale or pressure or scream that can match it.

When it's over, she gasps out a short sermon.

"Don't treat . . . people . . . this way. You'll harm yourself . . . in the . . . end. . . ."

"Ooooh!" The Head Labor Nurse lets out a little shriek. "Don't you threaten me! Get back there. March!"

"I can't walk."

"You walked out. Walk back."

By hobbles and crouches and creeping on fours, Hattie inches back. The squish and suck of gumshoes follows.

While she is creeping, she goes into one of those side-slipping episodes.

How it starts is that she's suddenly aware, while creeping, that her rough hospital shirt comes down only to the tops of her thighs. That its opening at the back is secured only with one tie. She is naked behind and shaved and naked in front. She understands she is ridiculous. The enema has been ridiculous. It has given her hard and painful cramps. She had squeezed down for nearly fifteen minutes to expel waste matter that was not there to be expelled. So has the shaving been ridiculous. It pricked and tickled and scraped along the tender inside of the lip until tears sprang to her eyes.

What can someone, who has just been given an enema and had her pubic hair shaved off and is crouching, nearly naked, say to the impeccably uniformed one?

The white uniform is beautifully starched. A bright blue-and-gold pin gleams on the shoulder of the uniform. The cap bears the stripe of rank and status. Hattie's shirt is of coarsest muslin, its wrinkles rough against her sweating skin. This is what they give the despised ones to wear. The paragon must be right. The despised ones in their despised clothes, with their disgusting excrements and their unsightly genitals, bleeding, gaping, oozing, squeezed, must be wrong.

I can't tell you how it happened, Jean. At that moment, the woman joined me, became me. Or I became her. We

*were the same person. I don't mean the Spanish Woman
in the Labor Room. I mean the other one. The one who la-
bored in the camp where there were typhoid lice in the
straw, on the cement, with the booted guard and the torch.
The one who squeezed her baby out into a world of concrete, straw and lice. . . .*

*At the same moment I could see, as if I were looking
at a series of those childbirth diagrams they showed at the
center, the whole thing of the baby's birth. First the baby,
when it's ready to be born, alerts the body. The body
clangs all its gongs, wrenches open all its locked places, un-
hinges all its doors. I could see the baby diving head fore-
most between Scylla and Charybdis, pubis and coccyx,
great stone defenders and crushers. It blocks with its head
the danger place. Then schemes and graces its body
through. Rolls over to its side to ease out shoulders. Then
face down again and the head push is back, up, out. Neck,
body and legs curve after. The baby swan-dives into air.
The first long swim complete. The first wet cry. The
first gulping of a life that at best, at best, will freeze, roast,
drench and finally desiccate this naked body, never to be
sheathed again except by earth, but a life that will also
permit it branches and bud, stem, leaves, root and flower
before the final frost. Into this life the baby dives. And
lands, under torch glare, in vermined straw, before the
booted feet. . . .*

By this time, and on such thoughts, Hattie had crept to
the door of the Labor Room. When she looked in, the Spanish Woman was gone. The bed was gone. She lifted her
head and howled: *Cursed be the booted feet. Cursed be the
legs that stood on them. Cursed and graveled be the groin,*

the belly, cursed be the leaded chest, cursed be the scoured brain through whose iron rafters echoed the baby's cry. Curse the Hun heart that shit on this grace!

Then they grabbed her.

Forty-four |

I peel the pages of Hattie's manuscript from my sweating fingers. I blow my nose, open a window, make a cup of tea. The little things that can be done to pass the time it takes for one particular moment to pass.

By the time I have drunk the tea, the moment is over. But before I can reach for your letter, there is one more thing I must know. What is the explanation for the questionnaire's being in my packet?

I thumb back through pages. I seem to have missed, here and there, more than I thought.

Here is the Labor Room again. "Help me, somebody." She vomits into a paper bag as the Spanish Woman had done. Each time a particular intern with sandy hair and glasses comes by she whispers, "Ezra?" He has asked for special permission to be present and shoot pictures but, like the obstetrician, he has not yet made it to the scene.

She is given an injection. Skip that.

She rants and calls and no one comes. Everything points to her having ceased to exist. Skip that.

Her bed is grabbed hold of and wheeled—under door

lintels, lights, past shadowy corners and more lights and then down a dim corridor of which the ceiling swims in purple motes—without a sound. Now she would know what had happened to the other woman and the other woman's bed. Now she, too, would be disposed of. I have already been in the Delivery Room. Skip that.

But here, suddenly is the Recovery Room. She asks for water, and a paper cupful is brought. She complains of a draft, and curtains are pulled around her bed. In her euphoria, as high as her despair was deep, she sees that somehow now that she needs less, is not crying or screaming out her needs, her privileges have been restored. She has regained status and can be considered human again.

Skip Ezra's exultant camera-clicking. Skip Lillian's tears and hugs. Skip Stanwood's also.

Now here is the angry stroke through the questionnaire. Hattie finishes the long indictment on the pulpy gray paper. She flings it on the supper tray and watches it, waiting for it to be picked up.

The thing is finished now and is on the tray, Jean. I'm waiting for it to be carried off by the nurse's aide. But such an overwhelming wish to have it back! Why? Somehow for the child's sake? But how would that affect . . . ? Somehow. Mother's superstition? Yes. Most beautiful and exalted thing. . . .

Hattie lies in bed, restless and exhausted. Then, as she hears the supper carts rattling in the hall, she snatches the paper back. She sends it—not to the authorities, but to me.

Hattie has broken through the mind-set. She has allowed herself to be diverted, to see the situation in a new way: 34-42-50-59-66-72. Not some implacable law whose code must be forced before anyone can take another step. Not at all. Relax, look at it, don't stare, hypnotized, but obliquely, corner of the eye, don't look at all, sniff it, don't even sniff it, let it suggest to you . . . is it, perhaps . . . can it be . . . is it possible . . . ?

This is the way to survive.

On another page it is all spelled out for me. . . . *As if somebody, somewhere, has opened the door a crack and something blows through the house like a draft. In spite of everything I know, it's joy.* . . .

It is now blue evening. It is time to know what is in the blue envelope.

Forty-five |

There are two separate sheets of writing paper, two idencal datelines, two identical salutations: "My dearest Jean—"

The first one:

"I'm filled with happiness. The decks are all cleared for us. Erna's going down to Alabama—that's the quickest way —and we can be married as soon as we get her wire that the divorce is granted. We're hurting no one now. This is how I prayed it would be. Erna wants me to tell you she wishes us both happiness. The children send you their love, as I do mine. . . ."

The second one:

"It's no good. Erna's having terrible depressions—under doctor's care and all of that. The younger children seem to have gone into shock. Ricky's dropped out of school and Marya has broken off with her fine young man because, she says, he'll only end up hurting her. I'm frightened for them all and I can't—under the circumstances—do anything more now about us. Do you see that, Jean? I'm miserable, but there's no point telling about that. I don't know whether it's weak or strong of me to give up what I want in order to try to keep my family afloat. But there's no point going into that either. . . ."

I have my large, working pocketbook, the one with all the zippered compartments, big enough to hold manuscripts. Into it I put your double letter and other things—a fat wallet, packs of cigarettes and tissues, paper and pencils, chocolate bars, Tampaxes. In case? Of what?

I keep throwing things into it until a knock at the door interrupts me.

"Look, I have brought us both a drink. In case you are not busy. I should have telephoned first. But I thought to myself, 'I must walk *out* of here or I will die,' eh? You know the feeling? But please, if I am interrupting something, tell me."

Sostana stands in the doorway with two brimming ice-filled glasses.

"No, I'm not busy. Only I may have to go out a little later. . . ."

She sinks into a chair and gives me a shrewd look. If she notices I have been crying she does not comment, any more than I would if I noticed she had been.

"He is upstairs in bed. My poor Mario. I think asleep. Such a tired big boy he was this evening. I gave him his dinner in bed and let him watch TV. He was asleep before his program was over. What joy when he sleeps."

She gives me her brilliant smile. "It is peaceful here. Thank you for letting me come in." A long sip and then rests her head against the back of the chair. "I am breathing again. Do you know where I went today with Mario? To the psychotherapist." She enunciates each word with scornful care. "This was an American one, and really quite a nice one. I have been before with Mario to European ones. They always want to take your life and sift through it grain by grain. I would rush to them with Mario in the middle of some crisis, the way you would rush to call the fire department, eh! if your house was on fire! But imagine if the fireman would say to you, 'I am so sorry, madam, about zis particular fire ve can nossing do—' her Italian accent stumbles into a German one—'but let us look carefully to see if ve can in ze future such fires prevent.' In the meantime, *Dio!* the house is burned to the ground. The Americans, on the other hand, are delightfully practical. They give concrete suggestions. Where to find listings of summer camps. What are good schools for the children. They are like friendly American Express agents. This one gave Mario some tests and afterward he spoke to me privately. He was truly concerned. He said to me, 'I know how hard you try. You are intelligent,' he said. 'I want to speak frankly. Mario must get away from you.'"

She takes a long drink and comes up out of it laughing her deep, scornful laugh. "'To where, to the moon?' I said. 'Am I supposed to send him there in a rocket?'

"'O no,' he said, 'there are wonderful boarding schools for boys, and many of the boys who go are of divorced parents. The school provides them with male parental figures and relieves them of the feeling that they are being disloyal to their fathers by spending so much time with their mothers. Then they can divide their vacations equally between both parents!'

"Then this very nice young American psychotherapist copied down for me the name of the book where all such schools are listed and he offered to speak to Mario's father and to convince him of the importance of such a move. So there you are, eh? *Dio!* What problems can there be now?"

After a moment Sostana asks me, without smiling, "Have you ever thought about suicide? No," she adds, "that's stupid of me. Of course everyone has thought of it. But I mean how you would do it? I have. I would send Mario to a good boarding school. Then I would write many, many letters which I would give to a friend to mail at intervals through the year, perhaps two years, or three. I would send a letter to the friend to say I have taken sleeping pills, and to please call the police. I would take them immediately after mailing the letter, so that by the time my friend received it she would already be too late. All through my letters to Mario I would be telling him, quite subtly, that the doctors say I have a little illness, not painful, with which I may live for many years, but that requires frequent rests and visits to doctors—and therefore I cannot visit him at school or have him home to visit me. All this time he would grow used to not seeing me, but he would also know that I was *there* and concerned for him."

"Do you *believe* this?"

"I would also buy birthday and Christmas presents for him, and little in-between presents, and they would be appropriate to Mario's interests and growth in the next few years, based on a kind of deduction from what he was when I saw him last. These presents would be sent by my friend also, over a period of years."

"But eventually he'd have to know."

"Yes, but by then, without his knowledge, he would have been prepared. And the grief would not be the kind from which a boy might not recover."

"But it would take such impossibly careful handling . . ."

"Yes, it would all depend on my letters and my friend."

"Do you even half seriously believe it might work?"

"Better than the other way. I have observed that even a most dependent child can learn to leave a parent. But he can never learn to tolerate a parent leaving him. And you?"

"Me?"

"Yes." She smiles conspiratorially. "I know it is morbid but come . . . let me play the psychotherapist for once. I now pronounce that it can sometimes be healthy to express one's morbid thoughts. What are yours? How would you . . . ?"

"I would choose a New York death."

"How delightful!" She laughs. "What is a New York death?"

"You enter Central Park at night. Have you ever done that?"

"No! *Dio!* Do you think I want to commit suicide?" Her husky laugh rings out.

"Sometime after dusk, when the park lights, haloed by fog, come on."

"O come! It sounds chilly, gloomy."

"No, beautiful. Fog, layers, depths of shadows and wavering lights. And silence. A floating mist above a sunken cathedral. Like wading into the sea."

"Death by drowning, then."

"No, not allowed. Whoever enters will be seized, pierced, parts ripped into." I sip calmly. "The classic city death."

"*Dio!* I will take my pills and go in peace." Sostana reviews my plan critically. "But suppose you are not seized? Or suppose you are seized, but still you survive? Then instead of your classic city death you will have been given only a ghastly experience."

"I will take along this interesting handbag—" I reach for my oversize one—"so obviously full of treasures. And of course I will guard it with my life."

"In that case—if I ever see you go out at night with that bag I will immediately call the police."

"And if you ever hand me a packet of letters addressed to Mario I will do the same."

"That would be wise."

We sip our drinks in a more-or-less peaceful silence. Sostana has made them strong.

After a moment she asks reflectively, "But really could you—the kind of woman you are—put yourself at the mercy, or the no-mercy, of whatever dreadful creatures there are, lurking in the park?"

"No, I couldn't go as I am. I would go as different people, at different stages of my walk."

"Who would you begin as?"

"At first, I suppose, standing before the stone entrance, I would feel myself a young girl. I would be sixteen, in a trench coat, hands in pockets, going out in the rain at night to meet a boy not approved of by my guardian. I would be going out to dangers I would never dare if not for my guardian's warnings and cries of alarm. My guardian, my aunt-mother, leaping ahead to bar my path and shrink my world, would also be there to protect me.

"During my walk across the park, I would age. I would remember the truth I learned later about her. I would think, 'Aunt, you gave me the false notion you were omnipotent.

I thought such a strong menacer as you would have divine powers over the world. But when I mutinied you melted away and left me powerless and alone.'

"I would become myself then. And frightened. 'I will make it to the other side of the park,' I will tell myself. 'I will come out all right there'—I would even be able to see the lighted towers ahead—'and take a cab home. Don't act silly,' I would tell myself. I would remind myself of who I am—a mature, professional woman, respected in her field and earner of a large yearly income. Inconceivable that I should sink into the mud, battered faceless, and left to decompose for a week behind bushes until some children, searching for their ball not far from the playground, find me.

"I would remember that I am now also God-mother to Hattie's child. There seems to be no transition from orphan to God-mother. I would hear scuffing in the bushes and tell my feet not to run. 'Walk steadily.' Footfalls will sound behind me. Someone inside me would whisper, 'God!' or 'Mother!' I would begin to run. Maybe at the very final moment I would remember that I am struggling toward the death I want, at the hands of someone whose loathing for his own life is as great as mine."

Sostana shudders. "*Dio!* That is enough therapy for now. We are both bursting with health."

Suddenly she lifts her face ceilingward and listens tensely. "Was that Mario?"

We both listen.

"Did you hear footsteps?" she asks.

"Nothing."

"Suppose he gets up and I am not there? Does it even matter? What can I do for him?"

"You would hear him."

She opens the door and walks a short way into the hall, listening for a sound from above.

"It is quiet. And even if it were not, I am not sure I would . . . She pauses on her way back. "What is this? Have you mail you don't know about?"

She comes in holding a large Manila envelope. It is dusty and shoe-printed. "It was peeping out from under your mat . . ."

I look at it but don't reach out for it.

"Don't you want your mail?"

"I can't believe it's more manuscript from Hattie. . . ."

Sostana laughs. "You don't have to read it if it is. But no, look, it has PHOTOS stamped on it."

We take it to my worktable, open it, shake it downward. The large, slippery 8 x 10 color photographs slide out.

Ezra has visited me. Here is his note. He was there with his equipment—special dispensation—in the Delivery Room. Either Hattie, in her semidrugged state, was unaware that Ezra was there, too, along with the smiling obstetrician, or she forgot and left it out, which seems unlikely, or I skipped over it. Ezra's note is triumphant. He is a father. Also this is the first time he has tried shooting anything like this. It turned out better than he expected and he has sent the whole series to a picture magazine. This set of prints is for me.

Here are the classic sights of birth: the great wound between the maternal thighs, the thick twisting cord; here are the doctor's hands inside wet rubber gloves, holding by ankles the limp, stunned animal.

Sostana's laugh begins again and rises almost to hysteria. "More . . ." she gasps out. "*Dio!* More babies . . .

give us more . . . endless babies . . . babies without end. . . ." Whisky splashes from her glass onto the prints. I snatch them away and without stopping to think what I am doing, I slip them into my large pocketbook and zip it shut. My bag is packed.

"I implore you, my dear friend—" Sostana is still laughing—"do not put anything more into that handbag while I am here."

"No, I won't." I put it on the floor near my desk.

Sostana sits down again. "To make sure you are not going out tonight with that bag, I'll ask you to refill my glass, please."

After a thoughtful pause over her drink she says, "Why do the two of us live like recluses? You devoted to your Loftus, I to my Mario? Why don't we plan, at least to travel one summer? Now that my nice American psychotherapist is going to speak to my ex-husband about finances, I really will have no more problem in that line. I will also have time if Mario will go to all these wonderful places the psychotherapist has in mind."

"You are forgetting one thing."

"Forgive me. Which thing?"

"I may be married by summer."

"In that case—" Sostana sips—"we would not go. Don't you think it might be amusing to plan anyway? It would only add to your pleasure if you were to cancel the plans."

Her frank glance shames me. She surely knows the possibilities.

"What on earth made me lie just now?"

"I am not addicted to 'the truth,' whatever that is," Sostana says calmly.

I reach for my bag.

"No, please," Sostana says in mock alarm.

"I want to show you something." I take the two letters out of their single envelope, unfold them and hold them out to her. I have a sense of betraying something, as in the moment when I blurted to the class the key to John Oates' false geometric progression, and for the same reason—to declare my position outside the mind-deceiving, locked pattern.

Sostana holds both letters before her and reads first one, then the other. Then she seems to read both simultaneously, as if they were one letter.

"He is imaginative," she murmurs. Then she glances quickly at my face. "Of course, my dear, I understand that you would have preferred one letter rather than two. Is he European?"

"No."

"I thought perhaps—because he sees the doubleness of things. But of course you want something clear-cut. You are right. He, on the other hand, is unable to separate what's in the egg. So he sends you the whole egg." She muses over the letters. "He is sensitive." Then glances back at me. "But of course you wanted him to send you a decision, not a dilemma. You are quite right. Perhaps he wants you to choose your own ending to the story?" She hands back the letters. I repack them in my bag.

"He has provided one ending for a romantic and one for a realist. Perhaps he is not certain which you truly are? One ending for the movies—as they say—and one for the book."

One for the money, two for the show, three to get ready and four to go.

Sostana gets to her feet. She, whose bodily movements are usually indolent, is suddenly full of resolve.

"I am going to slip upstairs for a moment. I will check on my Mario and I will bring down my box that is filled with little booklets and pictures and mementos of the places I have visited. The world is full of beautiful places. You will be the one to select whatever appeals most to you. It will pass the time—to make a plan—until we see which ending . . . ?"

When I hear that she has softly reached her door and opened it, I take my bag and slip out.

I walk the few blocks to the park, and enter. It is a cold clear night—starry and no moon.

I walk along a dim path that rises to a hill and then drops out of sight beyond its crest into the dark. There I will find them—Jesús' buddies, or the buddies of his buddies. The dispossessed ones who wait with pent-up rage. This is the path to take when I am ready to return their visits.

But it is not the path I take now.

Before it reaches the crest, the path forks. I follow the path that turns off to the right, at the end of which lights glow. It is not a long walk. But my handbag, full of possibilities, is a heavy weight. Either you will separate what's in the egg, Loftus, or you won't. Or I will travel with Sostana in the summer to the fascinating places women visit with other women. Or I will go back along the dark path that drops out of sight. . . .

I am on the terrace of rock overlooking the skating rink. I sit on a bench in the fogged lamplight, remove the photographs from my bag and study, in the dimness, what I had only hastily glanced at before with Sostana.

Here, on an aluminum table, under operation-theater lights and taken from various angles, lies the newborn daughter, big head veined and stained like a Tchelitchev baby's, one fist in the air, otherwise motionless, not crying, an infant lady, a Virgo in Aries at three in the morning, a strong, cleft girl, big-shouldered, bloody and calm. I kiss the bloody head. Welcome, God-daughter.

I put the pictures away and move to the edge of the terrace and look down. This is one of the last of the skaters' nights. Soon the rink will be shut down, though the air is still freezing. It will be spring.

I have to remind myself that it doesn't matter if, seen from this distance, the figures going around seem to have no meaning. And remind myself that when you are down there—in it—there is the excitement and warming rush of blood.

All the same, for a moment the skaters look insane. That laborious pushing around. Goal-less and circular. Endless and for what. As I gaze at them, nearly hypnotized, I discover there is nothing so difficult after all in this "passing through the membranes" that I thought was Hattie's specialty all this while. Stare at the skaters and soon, sure enough, the feeling of floating out beyond this accidental personal condition. Essence joins skaters. Wind-whipped in icy brightness. Going, stroking, leaning, keeling, pushing with tremendous effort and exhilaration under the stars that have already vanished and which now hold up their ghosts for us. See that couple, stumbling and laughing? I am hovering somewhere between, borne in a rush between their clasped hands. The organ crashes in. Some banal, exercising, potlid rhythm. And then, in spite of everything we know, the music makes us dance.

But Jesús is not here.

I turn away and back to the dark path. I am not seeking my fantasy death. If possible, I will avoid it. I am looking for Jesús, or the buddies of Jesús, who will have news of him. Of all the possibilities I carry with me, the one that draws me now is to find Jesús.

If I find him, and if he is willing, he will come into my house. I will adopt him—unofficially, if nothing more legal is allowed—and do us both great good. He will get from me books and money and hot showers, and he will bring me, without knowing it, whatever he remembers of his warm southern life. Do you believe me, Loftus, that I will ask no more of him than that? And if the worst should happen—some backsliding, an incident caused by his earlier association with bad companions—I will go to court for him. And weep, and tear my hair and shriek into the stern, judgmental faces: "He's a good boy! He would never do such a thing!"

It would be then as Hattie had described it—as if someone, somewhere, had opened the door a crack and something blew through the room like a draft. In spite of everything I know, it's joy and I cry, "He would never hurt anyone! God is my witness! He is good!"